GOLDFISH

—·—

HENRY WELLS

ROUGH PLACES PUBLISHING

First published 2025

ISBN: 978-1-7641038-0-0 (ebook)

ISBN: 978-1-7641038-1-7 (paperback)

It's all now you see. Yesterday won't be over until tomorrow and tomorrow began ten thousand years ago.

William Faulkner, Intruder in the Dust

Nothing brings memories to the surface like smells and flames.

Louis-Ferdinand Celine, Journey to the End of the Night

1

CHAPTER ONE

On the night that Peter Harrigan died, a man named Frank Corridini hit him across the back of the head with a claw hammer. He hit him just the one time, but he hit him hard, and the blow was enough to punch a hole in Harrigan's skull the size of a ten-cent piece.

Afterwards, when Harrigan had slipped off his chair to the concrete floor and a dark stain was spreading from his crotch, Corridini dug a cigarette from his shirt pocket and wedged it into the corner of his mouth.

He looked across the table at a large man sitting indifferently with an empty cup of coffee in front of him.

'If you want, I can hit him again,' he said.

The man was ill-lit by the bare light bulb hanging above the table. Only his resting hands and the partial shine of his bald pate showed amongst the shadows. He scraped his chair back, and the sickle-gleam of his head winked out as he straightened above the light's weak glare. He picked up a coffee pot and shook it to see what was left in the bottom.

'I'll let you be the judge of that,' he said. 'I'm going to toss these grinds.'

From the narrow strip of bushland across the road, the service station looked to be in darkness. A *CLOSED* sign hung crookedly in the doorway, and the petrol bowsers under the derelict canopy resembled stone obelisks in a country graveyard. A streetlamp a dozen metres down the road cast a sepia wash along the footpath that faded as it reached the forecourt. By the time the light touched the service station walls, it had become muted and illusory, like the smell of smoke in an empty room, tinged with disquiet and vague foreboding.

A door at the rear of the building swung open. The bald-headed man, whose name was Glover, stood in the pale rectangle of light. Glancing carelessly to his left and right, he trudged across the gravel to a waist high fence separating the service station from an adjoining paddock. There, he spilled the dregs from a coffee pot into the long grass beyond the fence. When it was emptied, he returned to the garage and, once inside, moved between two cars hydraulically raised above the grease-marked floor.

After setting the pot down on the table, he lent his hip against a workbench by the fridge and crossed his arms. Corridini, standing across from him, ran water into a battered steel basin and scrubbed blood spatter off his forearm. Glover waited for the water in the basin to run clear, then reached across, shut the taps off, and handed Corridini a towel to wipe his hands.

'You aren't up to this, you tell me.'

Corridini tossed the towel onto the bench. He rolled his neck, loosening the muscles in his shoulders, and met the bald man's flat, blue stare.

'I reckon I'll be alright.'

Fifteen minutes later, having lugged Harrigan across to the toilet block, they dumped his body in a shower recess and tore away the plastic sheet that shrouded him. Through a narrow breezeway high in the Besser block wall, cicadas chattered incessantly. Neither man spoke. Their boot heels scraped the floor as they stooped and grunted above their charge, sounding in the hollow room like lunatics shuffling in some dismal cellar of the damned.

Corridini stepped out of the recess. With more room to move, Glover set his feet apart and worked the belt loose from Harrigan's jeans. He tugged one boot off, then the other. On his knees then, his face flushed, he dragged Harrigan's pants down to his ankles and jerked them loose. He passed the jeans to Corridini. As he stepped back, Harrigan's legs fell heavily to the tiles. A naked woman with the face of a skull had been tattooed on his calf.

Corridini removed a wallet and a set of car keys from Harrigan's pockets. He dropped the jeans onto the floor and flipped the wallet open.

'What am I looking for?' he asked. Glover yanked a paper towel from the dispenser.

'You're smart, use your nut.' He wiped his hands, then folded the paper twice and daubed at his scalp. 'Look for receipts or ticket stubs. Anything that'll tell you where the money is.'

As Corridini went through the wallet, a slew of papers grew around his feet — random scraps, fugitive leavings. He noticed ripped fragments of a photograph wedged into a corner of the wallet. He dug the pieces out and reassembled them. A dark-haired woman wearing a loose halter top and carrying a baby stared back at him. The word 'cunt' had been written across her face.

Glover looked over his shoulder. 'And people reckon love's dead,' he said.

One other item in the wallet caught Corridini's attention. A dozen names and phone numbers scrawled on a page torn from a pocket notepad. *Tino, Luther, Chink, Mad Susan.* He passed the slip of notepaper to Glover and dropped the wallet onto the floor. 'That's it. Nothing to write home about.'

Glover glanced at the note. He shrugged, then handed it back. 'Leave it for now,' he said. Reaching across Harrigan, he spun the cold water tap on. The shower sputtered into life. Unbuttoning his shirt, he jutted his chin at the toilet block entrance. 'Grab your kit,' he said. 'The sooner we start, the sooner we finish.'

Corridini returned to the back of the garage. As he walked, the cicadas abruptly ceased their chorus and silence swelled around him. It was as if the night had been dropped into a void. The only sounds left in the world were the slow crush of his footsteps and the amplified throb of his pulse.

Inside the garage, he passed beneath the upraised vehicles. At the table where he had killed Harrigan, his shadow divided on the floor. He fancied he could hear the sound of his boots continuing across the concrete. As the sound diminished, a tapping noise replaced it. It took Corridini a second to realise that the sink tap was still dripping.

From a darkened space beneath the workbench, he drew out a canvas satchel and placed it amongst the abandoned beer bottles on the table. A row of empty paint tins stood against the wall. Corridini retrieved one of the tins and stood with it dangling in his hand. The tin's weightlessness caused him to feel momentarily giddy. He closed his eyes and waited for the feeling to pass.

Harrigan balanced his weight on the back legs of his chair. There were a pair of tallies standing empty on the table in front of him. He opened a fresh bottle.

Behind him, Corridini picked distractedly at the Fourex label on his own bottle. He glanced at the clock. 6:49. A watched clock never moves.

Harrigan lit a cigarette. After dropping the matchhead into one of the empties, he took a deep drag and blew the smoke into his lap.

'Where was I?' he asked.

At the other end of the table, Glover sat with his chair turned about. He poured coffee into an enamel cup. 'Women are fucking bitches,' he said.

Harrigan's teeth showed. 'That's right, fucking Raelene. Last Wednesday, she grabbed the kid and called me a fucking psycho. Left me sitting there like a dickhead. You've got no idea what a fucking nutcase she is.

'Anyway, I put the telly on, thinking I'll watch the cricket. No such luck. There's Richie Benaud looking like someone drowned his mother. Half a foot of water's on the pitch. I clicked through the channels. Nothing on but fucking Columbo.'

He flicked ash at the table. 'Ever watch that show? Derro cop, looks like he sleeps under a bridge?'

Glover stirred his coffee. 'All I got's a wireless.'

'Well, you aren't missing anything. I did a half-dozen cones, and it was still shit. The copper looks like a metho drinker. I'd give him less than a minute with those cunts from Special Branch. They'd kick seven colours of shit out of him before he knew what day it was.'

On the bench beside Corridini sat a state-of-the-art Kenwood car cassette radio and the headlight assembly of a 1976 Nissan 610. There was also a straight claw hammer with True Temper markings stamped into its brown rubber grip.

The clock on the wall read 6:55.

Harrigan dropped the front legs of his chair onto the concrete. He stubbed his cigarette out with the heel of his boot, then tapped the light bulb above his head with a tobacco-stained finger.

Suddenly, the room lost its equilibrium. Shadows leapt and lunged about the walls. Corridini set aside his beer bottle. He stared at the light as the room went in and out of focus.

When the bulb settled, Harrigan rubbed a scarred knuckle into one of his reddened eyes. A look of great weariness passed over his face. 'You know what?' he said. 'I feel well and truly fucked.'

When he re-entered the toilet block, Corridini halted. Grunts and obscenities were issuing from the end stall. In the fly-spotted glass of the mirror a strange tableau of limbs greeted him.

Glover was straddling Harrigan in the shower stall, pinning him to the tiles with his elbow. The smaller man had come to life and was convulsing and heaving beneath him. Blood streamed from Harrigan's fractured skull and the water around him curdled a vivid pink. Scrabbling violently, he wrapped Glover's midriff with his legs and, rising up, sank his teeth into the big man's neck.

Over it all, the shower water streamed, cloaking the scene in a grey mist that disembodied the men, making a grotesque pantomime of their struggle.

Corridini dropped his paint tin onto the tiles. He cast about inside the satchel until his fingers fell on the walnut grip of a 9mm Browning. Drawing the pistol out, he braced himself against the side of the stall. Then he lent past Glover's shoulder and stuck the gun barrel into Harrigan's eye.

'Jesus, Pete. How fucking hard does this have to be?'

Half-naked in sodden pants, Glover dried himself with a towel from Corridini's satchel. Blood spatter coated his face and teeth marks scored his neck. The gunshot had partially deafened him and he shook his head to clear it. When he spoke, his voice was unnaturally loud. 'Next time,' he said, 'we'll do things differently.'

Corridini collected Glover's shirt from the floor and handed it to the older man. Muddied boot prints dirtied the tiles from one end of the toilet block to the other. 'You're bleeding,' Corridini said.

'What's that?'

'I said, you're bleeding.'

In the fleshy part of Glover's palm, a gaping wound made by Harrigan's teeth dripped blood onto the tiles. The big man raised his hand and inspected it. 'Bastard bit me like a mongrel dog.'

Harrigan's clothes lay piled where Corridini had dropped them. He handed the dead man's t-shirt to Glover, who used the fabric to bind his hand. When he finished, he stepped into his trousers and pulled his boots on. Then he moved past Corridini to the sink nearest the entrance.

'Give us the cunt's keys,' he said. 'I'll take a quick look at his shitbox, then I'll give Victor a ring.'

Corridini lifted his eyes to the toilet block ceiling. The unnatural light of the fluorescent tube evoked strong memories. Hospital wards, train stations, abattoirs. Places of loneliness and pain.

He stripped to his underwear. *You killed a man, what the fuck do you expect?*

Skull fragments lapped around him in the shower stall. He pulled a 25-inch stainless steel bone saw from the canvas folds of his satchel, then dropped the satchel outside the stall.

Until a year and a half ago, he had spent his days on an abattoir floor.

Dangling beasts the size of small Japanese cars were dismantled under a clamorous factory roof. The work resembled an automobile production line thrown into hard reverse. When they were finished, nothing remained of the slaughtered beasts — save the pervasive and ineradicable odour of their fear.

Corridini set his feet apart. It's amazing what you can do if you set your mind to it.

When Glover returned to the toilet block, Corridini didn't look up. His mind was elsewhere, rambling down old pathways.

The shape of his father's felt hat. His mother's coffin. A 16-ton Bedford lorry with the door open; a transistor radio playing tinnily on the dash.

He shifted position in the stall and turned Harrigan's torso on its side.

Displaced water sloshed about the recess. He used his knee to hold Harrigan's body in place. With the bone saw cradled in one arm, he reached into the crimson water and unclogged the drain.

A great gurgling ensued. He rested on his haunches, closed his eyes, and let his head fall forward on his chest.

Glover watched him disinterestedly. At the edges of his mouth, a tautness showed. He cleared his throat. 'You didn't bleed him,' he said.

Corridini opened his eyes. Without looking around, he gestured at Harrigan's ruined skull. 'There didn't seem to be much point.' Tipping his head back, he washed the blood off his chest and arms. He spoke above the shower: 'What about you? How did you go?'

Glover inspected the back of his good hand. 'So, so,' he said.

Corridini pushed to his feet. He rinsed the blood from his legs, then turned the shower off. Stepping out of the stall, he accepted the towel Glover handed him.

'You didn't find the money?'

Glover shook his head. 'It'll turn up.'

'Did you talk to Victor? What does he say?'

'Victor doesn't say anything. I haven't called him yet.'

Corridini dried his hair, then paused and lowered the towel. 'He said to ring by eight.'

Glover appeared not to have heard. He took Harrigan's car keys from his pocket and turned towards the door. 'Put your pants on,' he said. 'I want to show you something.'

Outside, headlights swept the scrubland on the western perimeter of the service station. The two men paused. Phantom lights danced among the tree trunks, car tyres rattled the graded road fifty metres away. The sound diminished into the distance.

Corridini followed the pale dome of Glover's bald head. As they walked, the big man flipped Harrigan's car keys into the air. Once, twice, a flash of silver catching the moonlight.

As they approached Harrigan's tan '74 Corolla hatchback, Corridini's step faltered. Like a man moving towards a sheer drop, his equilibrium tipped and veered. Old dreads surfaced. He clenched his hands into fists and felt the tendons in his arms pop up.

Glover rounded the Corolla. After opening the driver's door, he stepped back, then beckoned Corridini nearer with his injured hand. 'For Christ's sake, Frank,' he said. 'She isn't going to bite.'

Strapped into a booster seat in the back of the Corolla was a three-year-old girl. Her head lolled insensibly to one side. A cotton sheet half-draped her thin legs. As Corridini peered in from the driver's door, the sheet fell away, slipping into the dark recess at her feet.

The overhead light dimmed. Corridini dug his lighter from his pocket and snapped it on. The young girl's face jumped and wavered into view. He lent awkwardly past the driver's seat, holding his breath like a pilgrim catching sight of a new Jerusalem.

The cabin's interior smelled of urine and lighter fluid. Corridini exhaled. As the seconds passed, the brass casing of his Zippo grew hot in his hand. He held onto it as long as he could, then shook it out. The child's face dissolved into darkness before him. Slowly, he backed away from the car.

Glover was leaning against the bonnet. The expression on his face sent something slick and cold scurrying down Corridini's spine.

Glover placed a cigarette between his lips, then cupped his injured hand around a flaring match. He shook the flame out. 'So, you've seen her,' he said.

Corridini looked down at the darkened windscreen. 'Yes, God help us.'

Glover tilted his head back and narrowed his eyes. 'Old Pete's full of surprises.'

A wave of nervous energy flooded through Corridini's body. 'Jesus Christ, Lucas. He's a fucking psychopath.'

'Well then.'

'Everything's turned to shit. What the fuck was he thinking?'

Glover cocked his head to one side. He pointed at his deafened ear. 'Speak up,' he said.

Corridini jammed his hands into his pockets to keep them still. He stood so Glover could see his mouth and lips moving. 'If we're not careful,' he said, 'she'll spew and choke to death on her own vomit.'

Glover's eyes grew still. He tapped the ash off the end of his cigarette and blew on the tip. A red glow expanded, lighting his face and hand. 'That doesn't need to be the end of the world, now does it?'

Before leaving for the service station that afternoon, Corridini field dressed the 9mm Browning in the bedroom of his small flat.

Sitting on an old chrome and vinyl chair, he ejected the weapon's cartridge onto his bedspread, then slid back the slide, checking he didn't have a round in the chamber. Finding it clear, he thumbed the safety on, then released the slide lock from the frame, and disassembled the pistol onto the faded chenille cover in front of him.

After taking down the gun, he wiped and oiled each part separately, using a soft cloth, and a piece of cord to clean the barrel. A droplet of sweat gathered on the end of his nose. He wiped it away. Bars of sunshine fell across him from the louvres.

He did his best to clear his mind. Picture a spot on the wall. Let it narrow to a point until it vanishes. Focus only on the thing in front of you.

Everything Corridini knew about the gun had been taught to him by Victor Keats. He knew the pistol could bite the webbing of a shooter's thumb when it was fired. He also knew that the hammer could be tricky to cock. The last thing Victor told him was to always carry the Browning in 'Condition One'.

'Condition One?' Corridini asked.

'That's right,' Victor said. 'The Yanks call it 'cocked and locked'.'

He held the firearm up, racked the slide so that the hammer cocked, then used his thumb to press the safety on. 'When you carry it, carry it like this. Don't stuff around.'

Corridini accepted the gun. He felt its weight in his hand, then extended his arm, pointing the barrel at the ground.

'Safety off,' he said. 'Point. Shoot.'

Victor grinned. A black space showed where one of his teeth was missing.

'Jesus, Frank. You're a bloody natural, you are.'

Entering the toilet block again, Corridini lagged a pace or two behind Glover. The big man preceded him to the sink, where he pulled back his collar to examine the bite mark Harrigan had made in his neck. Misshapen teeth, a florid circle, angry bruising.

Corridini slipped behind him. He crouched at the satchel and opened its canvas flap. He found the Browning 9mm where he had left it after shooting Harrigan. It was 'cocked and locked', the way he'd been taught. Rising, with the gun against his side, he thumbed the safety off. Then he turned and stepped towards Glover, raising his arm in a single motion.

The big man caught Corridini's movement in the glass. His pale blue eyes shifted focus, giving him just enough time to register the gun's muzzle before Corridini shot him in the back of the skull.

2

CHAPTER TWO

O n the wall by the door connecting the garage to the service station's
front shop, the phone was ringing. Corridini stumbled toward it.
A raised car loomed either side of him and he ducked to avoid banging
his head. He lifted the hand piece and listened.

'Who's this?' a voice asked.

'It's me,' said Corridini.

'Who the fuck's 'me'? Is that you, Frank?'

'That's right, Mr Keats.' He looked down at his dishevelled self. His
fly unbuttoned, the cuffs of his trousers crumpled over his boots.

Victor Keats' voice crackled in his ear. 'You must think I'm some sort
of drongo. You don't think I have anything better to do than sit around
waiting for you to ring.' Corridini wound the handset cord around his
finger.

'Something came up,' he said.

'Is Lucas there?'

'I left him out back. We've still got some tidying up to do.'

'If I was in Brisbane, I'd come out,' said Keats.

Corridini looked at his finger. The flesh around his nail had darkened and started to swell. He closed his eyes, focusing on the sensation.
'There isn't any need,' he said.

'Tell me you got this, Frank.'
'We've got it, Mr Keats. Everything's under control.'

In the hour before daybreak Corridini sat at the cluttered table. His hands draped motionlessly between his knees, one of Harrigan's cigarettes burning in his left hand.

He'd been sitting here off and on since midnight. Smoke from the cigarette reddened his eyes. He squinted through the haze at his fingers, at the blood crusted under his nails. A neat cylinder of ash fell from the end of his cigarette.

He made a sucking noise with his teeth, then scraped his boot across the floor and ground the ash into the concrete.

'Amen,' he said.

Packed into heavy garbage bags, the dead men were piled in pieces on a paint spattered canvas sheet by the garage door. Bundled organs, severed tendons, jointed limbs. The pile shifted and settled like a mal-odorous beast slumbering on a bone-strewn floor.

In a space amongst the empty beer bottles on the table sat the paint tin he had taken from beneath the bench the night before. Another tin of equal size sat beside it. Between these tins Corridini had placed a box of two-inch nails.

Corridini dropped his cigarette into the neck of an empty bottle, then tipped the box onto its side. A dozen nails spilled out like runes onto the tabletop. He sorted through them with his fingertips.

Around Corridini the night beat a slow retreat. Hulking shapes resolved themselves from the darkness. Waste oil tanks. An engine stand. A pair of Holden bucket seats. Outside, birdcalls, arcane and eerie, rasped and cawed in the surrounding scrub.

The wall clock read 4:10. He slipped another Winfield from Harrigan's packet.

Leaving the table, he crossed to the fridge and pulled a tall Fourex from the bottles racked in the door. He twisted the top off, then sucked away the suds. A dull pain stabbed his temples.

On the canvas sheet by the garage door, one of the bags slumped sideways. Corridini lifted his bottle and drank.

Back at the table, he lit the Winfield. Pinching the filter between his thumb and middle finger, he watched Harrigan's daughter sleeping on a camp bed between the bench and an old filing cabinet.

He'd carried her in from the car after killing Glover and her father. Now, the girl lay sheathed like a ghost behind the exhaled smoke of his cigarette.

Using the True Temper claw hammer he'd bludgeoned Harrigan with, Corridini punched a nail into the side of one of the tins. He worked the nail free, then tapped in a second hole. He smoked his cigarette down to the filter.

More holes appeared in the tin, randomly placed. Ten, fifteen, twenty. Periodically, he lowered the hammer and studied his progress in the weak light of the hanging bulb.

Perspiration beaded Corridini's forehead. After a time, the sweat coalesced and ran down his temples. He dragged a sleeve across his brow and kept working.

By the time he finished, dawn had worked its way into the garage and a muted half-light was bleeding through the gloom.

Corridini set his tins on the table and sat back. Hundreds of perforations, each with a thin skirt of tin punched inwards, covered the circumference of both tins. With their lids batted firmly closed, they'd fill quickly with water and sink.

Corridini scrubbed his face. 'God save me.'

Muted yellow light filtered through a row of cobwebbed louvres to his left. He twisted in his chair, squinting at them. Dust mites swayed in the shimmering haze like angels cut loose from heaven.

An image of Corridini's uncle.

The old man sits shirtless at a kitchen table. A white singlet covers his broad, grey-haired chest. Black eyes burn up at the ceiling. The knuckles of his work-broken hands show white as he clenches and unclenches his fists in strained, barely controlled fury.

In the background, Corridini's aunt, the old man's wife, sits obscured by the sun at her back. She reads passages from a vellum-covered Bible in a savage and bitter voice.

'And the Lord God took the man and put him in the garden of Eden to till it and to keep it. And the Lord God commanded the man, saying, 'Of every tree of the garden thou mayest freely eat: but of the tree of the knowledge of good and evil, thou shalt not eat of it: for in the day that thou eatest thereof thou shalt surely die'.'

Corridini crossed the garage floor. As he ducked beneath one of the raised cars, the strength dropped out of his legs like water tipped from a bucket. He waited a moment, then went on.

At the paint-spattered sheet, his hands shook as he fumbled through the charnel waste. He clasped and prodded bags until he found the two he was looking for. After clearing a space on the table-top, he opened the first of the bags. Glover's face, nestled in plastic, stared back at him.

In death, the bald man's expression retained its cold certainty. Rigor mortis had hardened his jaw askew. One greyish blue eye condemned the world from beneath a partially open lid.

In the small brick and fibro flat where Corridini lived, his bedroom walls were bare except for a half-length mirror and an Escher print stuck to the wall with blu tack. Corridini had bought the print on an impulse at a garage sale two years earlier, while buying an iron skillet and a stainless-steel pot for his kitchen. It depicted anonymous cowled figures climbing and descending a set of stone steps in endless repetition. When looked at closely, the steps went neither up nor down, and the men trudging them were trapped in an exquisitely futile endeavour.

Every morning Corridini lay in bed, studying that poster. Some days he felt giddy looking at it, as if the world were sliding around beneath his feet. Other days the room itself became part of the picture. When that happened, he sensed himself on the verge of a deep realisation that never quite clicked into place.

It took him three attempts to fit Glover's head fully into the first paint tin. Sticky with blood, he wiped his hands on an old rag, then coaxed Harrigan's head into the second tin with greater ease. Afterwards, he took a bottle of beer from the fridge and retreated to the furthermost corner of the garage. There, he slumped to the floor and lent against a tier of radial tyres.

Through the night abrupt and painful visions visited him, flaring behind his eyeballs like zirconium flashes in a closed and empty room.

He saw Harrigan rocking on the hind legs of his chair, thirty-two years of hatred infusing his veins.

'I tore the screen door off its hinges. Try to lock me out, will you, you cunt?'

The light bulb veered crazily.

In that instant Corridini heard the sharp report of his hammer meeting the crown of Harrigan's head.

Ripples of violence radiated outwards. An electrical charge burned up his arm.

A vision of orange silk unfurled behind his half-closed eyes.

Pedestrians jostled on a footpath. A woman walked through a crowd with her scarf flowing behind her. The silk undulated. It found shadows in the sunshine and blended them into a lush crimson colour.

Corridini lent against the stacked tyres. He tasted the hammer blow with his clenched back teeth.

A boot seemed to have been placed on his chest.

He gasped and sat heaving for air. His hands flapped in his lap. He pressed them into his legs, trying to calm himself.

On the floor of Corridini's flat was a loop pile carpet. Laid sometime in the middle 1960s, every square inch of it was covered with cigarette burns.

The burns had been made by the flat's previous tenant, a fifty-year-old Scrumpy drinker, dying of cirrhosis, with an above-knee amputation and no feeling in his fingers.

The tenant had passed out in every corner of the flat — under the phone table, behind the Naugahyde couch. Wherever he fell, he burned a narrow black mark into the orange Bergen carpet.

Seemingly, his mission in life was to pattern the floors with these strange hieroglyphics. Using the burn marks, perhaps, to record his mad and inchoate ramblings, or to preserve a fevered mathematical reckoning of his nightmare existence. Some men constructed houses out of empty beer and wine bottles. Others burned their misery and pain into the fibres of an orange carpet.

In the garage, Corridini pictured himself on his bed with the sun on his back. He imagined its warmth on his neck and arms and summoned from memory an image of the carpet spreading out from his feet.

He studied it, letting his eyes feel their way over the pattern of burn and anti-burn, of carpet and not-carpet, of darkness and light. Gradually, the burn marks swam together. Then a breeze seemed to take them, and they expanded outwards like ripples on a pond.

Through closed eyelids, Corridini saw orbs of colour grow out of the darkness and knew that the sun had driven what was left of the night into the cracks and nether parts of the world.

Above him, the garage lay in vast somnolence. Great shadows dripped in torpor from the walls as if the entire chamber was sagging in the summer heat.

Corridini's lips trembled. Except for the buzzing of flies, the garage remained silent.

A breeze stirred across the high corrugated iron roof and with it, leaves went rustling drily in the gutters. The ancient rafters groaned, resigned, as the growing heat swelled the metal struts that crisscrossed the walls like a primitive lattice.

Corridini opened his eyes. He shifted his head, staring into the murky gloom. A rustle of movement scuffed the concrete floor somewhere across from him. It came from the darkened recesses beyond the up-raised chassis of the cars.

Scrsk. Scrsk.

In a dusty interstice of light, he saw it: a glimpse of light-coloured fabric, washed out and blue. It rippled once in the sloping light, then disappeared.

Images of dead men reared. First Harrigan, then Glover.

Protoplasmic forms constructed of shadow and light. They dipped and weaved above the pile of their own mortal parts, shipwreck survivors broken-limbed on a desolate shore.

Corridini rubbed his eyes with the heels of his hands. When he looked again, the phantoms were gone. In their place, the mote-filled light swayed above the concrete floor, lighting one side of the canvas sheet and the corrugated garage wall beyond it.

Ducking his head beneath the first car, he saw the girl. She stood in the gauzy light at the edge of the canvas, her foot centimetres from the garbage bags in which portions of her father lay.

Corridini stood perfectly still. The sound of his breath burned in his ears. In the half-light, the girl's eyes were hooded and sallow. She had crossed the floor in her sleep.

A dark puddle slowly expanded around her feet. It spread outwards, until it met the piled canvas, where it redirected in runnels along the cement. When she finished, her legs and the hem of her skirt were splashed with urine.

Corridini felt a plunging sense of loneliness in his chest. He found himself at the precipitous edge of his own childhood. A primal and instinctive fear seized him. His childhood wasn't a place he wanted to go.

The girl felt hopelessly small in his arms. Against his chest, he could feel the birdlike flutter of her heart. He cradled the back of her head with the palm of his hand and caught the dusky smell of her drugged body and hair in his nose.

He dragged the cot away from the filing cabinet. Then he bent and untangled the girl's arms from his neck, letting her legs and torso find their way onto the cot.

When he released her, she dropped into herself like someone falling backwards into water. Her head lolled to the side. Drool shone on her lip.

Corridini looked up at the wall clock. 7:45. The second hand jerked mechanically around the dial like a lame man's leg. For a moment he forgot where he was.

A year earlier.

Glover tried to dislodge a piece of food caught between two of his back teeth with his fingers. He was loitering in the little fibro hall outside Corridini's room while the younger man changed out of a bloodied t-shirt. Glover wiped his fingers with a handkerchief. He folded it and tucked it back into his pocket, probing the inside of his mouth with his tongue.

Corridini jiggled a cupboard drawer open. He found a t-shirt and took it from the folded pile. As he pulled the shirt over his head, he noticed Glover's eyes drawn to the Escher print on his wall.

'What do you think?' he asked.

'Not much.'

'You've seen pictures like it before?'

'Hippy shit,' said Glover. 'Salvador Dali. Lava lamps. The Grateful Dead.'

Corridini grabbed his wallet from the bedside table. 'Some sheila in Runcorn sold it to me. I wanted something for the wall.'

Glover gave the monk-like figures a last glance. He peeled his lip back and ran his tongue over his teeth. 'They look like fucking mugs to me.'

Corridini rolled the girl onto her side. He pulled the cotton sheet away and dumped it onto the floor. Clumsily, he undressed the girl.

When he was finished, he tossed her wet skirt and underclothes onto the concrete next to the cot. At the sink, he filled a bucket with warm water and grabbed a tea towel from the draining board. Then he carried the bucket back to the cot, water splashing onto the floor as he went.

After carefully wiping down the child's body, he recovered the sheet from the floor and gently wrapped her in it. He emptied the bucket into the sink and returned to the table. He sat with his chair turned about, facing the tiny figure on the cot, his shadow spilling across the floor towards her.

Corridini shifted a cardboard box from the floor by his foot. In the box were the clothes Glover and Harrigan were wearing when he killed them.

On top of the pile were the girl's things. A small dress, three t-shirts, a pair of shorts with a flower sewn onto the pocket, and two changes of underwear. There was also a pair of yellow thongs small enough for Corridini to fit side-by-side on the flat of his hand.

Nestled with the clothes was a pill bottle. Corridini reached into the box and took the pill bottle out. He turned it on its side and counted eight tablets sliding around inside the glass.

The pills had been on the back seat of Harrigan's Corolla. He had found the bottle with the clothes when he went back to the car. Now, he held it up so light could catch the label. *Nitrazepam*. Otherwise known as Mogadon. 5mg a tablet.

At the bottom of the label, written in spidery blue ink, an initial and a surname. *Ms. R Tillich*.

The night before, while going through Harrigan's wallet, he remembered the scraps of photograph he'd found hidden in its folds. Raelene Tillich squinting quizzically into the sunlight. Her daughter in her arms. The word 'cunt' scratched onto her face.

A shadow loomed beside him. Glover gave the photograph a cursory glance.

'Love's dead', he said, then walked off into the night.

The tiled floor stretched into the distance. The earth curved. Straight lines converged. Day became night. Night became day.

In Corridini's mind the tiles were replaced by a cracked linoleum floor. Harrigan hunched at a low teak veneer coffee table. He crushed a tablet into powder with a butter knife. When he was done, he tapped the powder into a glass of orange juice and stirred the juice with the blade.

Across the table the girl sat watching in dumb misery. He pushed the glass toward her.

'For fuck's sake, your mother's not coming. Go on, we're not leaving till you drink it.'

Corridini popped the top off the pill bottle. He shook a pill into his hand and tipped it onto the table.

'Jesus, Pete. How the fuck did we end up here?'

3

CHAPTER THREE

*C*orridini didn't remember much about his parents. A few vague fragments. Like lights bobbing on a flooded river. Oddments, varied and strange, soundlessly passing into a black and cavernous void.

He recalled smells and sounds. Sometimes the reflection in someone's eye conjured an image of his mother. Other times, a tune half heard on a radio recalled his father to him. He heard whistling in a room. The tap of a razor on the porcelain edge of a yellowed sink. The dip and creak of a mattress. The smell of stockings drying on a towel rail.

Sometimes he imagined his mother's warm hand pressed against his cheek. He'd close his eyes and imagine her beside him. He felt like a figure listening at a locked door, trying to hear beyond it – the sound of breathing or the shuffle of movement in an unreachable room.

His parents died on a Friday morning, just before midday. Their deaths were sudden and catastrophic. The papers called them an act of God.

Corridini was six days past his fifth birthday. It was as if a tidal wave had washed them away. One minute they were beside him on the footpath; the next, they were gone.

They were waiting for the 591 tram to pass. The City Hall clock pealed the three-quarter hour mark. Above the traffic din, pigeons broke noisily from eaves and gutters, scattering into the air.

Corridini wore a tie, a replica of his father's. Thin and black, with a tiny anchor at the point. Holding his mother's hand, he raised his foot and scratched the back of his calf with the toe of his shoe.

A boy on the tram watched Corridini through a closed side window. Beside him, partially visible through the same window, sat a hatted man. He bent his head to the boy's ear and whispered to him fiercely.

Corridini, still gripping his mother's hand, stood transfixed by the man's lips, which fluttered and curled like a fat woman's fingers.

The traffic light changed. The tram clanged forward. As it turned, the hatted man slipped from sight like something reptilian pulled back into a fetid pond.

The two boys contemplated one another as the distance grew between them. Corridini wondered if he and the boy knew each other. How else could he explain the sudden, sickening ache in his heart?

Corridini felt divided and lost. As if someone had stolen his reflection. As if a part of him had become a ghost.

On the sun-washed footpath, with their shadows gathered close around their feet, Corridini and his parents walked north along Queen Street.

They crossed at an intersection. A throng of people bustled near. His mother stopped suddenly, bringing a hand to her face. She clutched her husband's arm.

'Harry, stop a second. There's something in my eye.'

People jostled past. Corridini tipped his head back. He turned in a narrow circle. The earth wobbled on its axis.

A great yellow crane, bridging the space between two buildings, darkened the sun. Corridini saw spots in front of his eyes. A whistle sounded, shrill and terrible, the screech of a giant metal bird.

Above the city noise, his mother's voice sounded sharp with impatience. 'Harry, pay attention, there's something in my eye.'

Corridini reached for her hand. A widemouthed woman with a small, perfectly shaped mole in the dimple of her smile looked down at him in surprise.

'Where did you come from?' she asked.

The woman wore a white dress covered in hibiscus flowers. Her eyes were shaded by a broad summer hat. A loose orange scarf worn lightly around her white neck drew attention to the tendons beneath the clean perfection of her skin. Her eyes sparkled and the mole moved charmingly. She released his hand from her wrist, and he watched her slip away like a boat drawn downstream by the current of a river.

'If you take your hands away,' his father said, 'maybe I can see to help.'

Corridini's eyes followed the scarf. Briefly, a man's hand brushed his shoulder. He felt himself gently guided forward by the pressure. His feet moved mechanically.

Ahead, the scarf undulated, beguiling as an ocean. Corridini's steps quickened.

And then the world cleaved in two. A tremendous, deafening crash filled the air and the footpath convulsed. Corridini covered his ears. Day transmogrified into night.

A strange metamorphic dream unfolded around him. He hovered in a brown light. All of his orifices were clogged with dust. Gradually the world emerged like a sepia image from a chemical bath.

A woman missing the heel of her shoe stumbled passed him. Her eyes were fixed on a point above one of the sandstone buildings.

Corridini followed her gaze. He expected to see a herald of angels in the sky. All he saw was dirt and cement dust, and the dirty smear of the sun.

A man in a grey fedora stepped off the footpath. He took a handkerchief from his pocket and spread it on the curb. With a strangely dignified air, he sat carefully down on the handkerchief and covered his face with his hands.

'Suddenly I'm very small.

'I'm sitting in the gutter looking at a lorry idling in the middle of the road. The driver's nowhere in sight. I can see his keys dangling from the ignition. The lorry doors have been flung open as if a bomb exploded inside the cabin.

'There's a man sitting next to me with his face in his hands. I want to ask him if he knows where my mother is.'

A transistor radio on the dashboard played Cinderella Rockafella: 'I love your jazz. Razza-ma-tazz. I love your jazz-a-razza-ma-tazz'.

People screamed.

Corridini put his fingers in his ears. His teeth chattered.

Next to the lorry's front tyre, a sheaf of papers fastened to a clipboard riffled in a breeze. Dust swirled and fell away. The pages jerked and flapped like an injured bird's wing.

The lorry stood covered in grey dust.

Corridini wanted to be sick.

There was nothing inside him but dust.

The fluorescent light in the toilet block buzzed and flickered. Corridini, naked except for his underpants, stood above Glover's remains in the shower stall. His face was set in an immutable mask. At his throat a nerve fluttered, hazy and intermittent.

Bending down, he tore a garbage bag from the package by his feet and snapped it open. With his other hand, he seized hold of Glover's foot, lifting it quickly from the pile and feeding it into the bag. His expression did not falter.

The newspapers had a hard time containing themselves. No sooner had the dead been pulled from the rubble than copy editors devised lurid banner headlines for their morning editions.

'Act of God.' 'Death from Above.' 'The Day the Earth Stood Still.'

Speculation ran riot. Scapegoats were sought. Allegations surfaced of a Labor Party cover-up. Siphoned union funds, corrupt land deals. Rumours circulated of a Texas millionaire with shady business connections.

The truth was more prosaic.

A reinforced concrete slab, too heavy for the harness supporting it, fell four stories onto a crowded lunchtime footpath. When the site foreman heard the screams, he dropped his clipboard and left the building site. They found him drunk in a public toilet by the river. He was sitting in a cubicle with his shoes and socks off.

Two weeks later, he drove his '64 Fairlane into a cattle truck on the Cunningham Highway.

Corridini's uncle kept the old newspapers in a shed on his farm. Piled in mouldering stacks, they went back twenty years to the Queen's coronation.

One winter Corridini sorted through them. August 1974. The cold ate into his bones, and his feet felt like wooden clogs in the outsize galoshes his uncle had given him to wear.

Corridini didn't let the cold affect him. He found a way to put his feelings aside — to watch them the way you'd watch a fire burning.

In one of the papers, he saw a photograph. The place where his parents died. The rubble had been cleared away. A cordon erected. Tributes left on the footpath. Wreaths and cards and small mementoes. Like the personal effects of passengers washed ashore after a ship goes down.

A policeman guarded the makeshift shrine. On the road, a crowd looked on. Between the crowd and the policeman stood a young boy and a late middle-aged woman.

Corridini recognised himself. The woman beside him was his aunt. She wore a drab colourless dress and a pair of square-toed, mannish shoes. In her hands, she clasped a plain brown handbag.

Neither Corridini nor his aunt looked at the tributes. Instead, their eyes were directed elsewhere. Corridini's at a place near his feet. His aunt's, at a point somewhere beyond the photographer's frame. Her mouth was fixed in a thin, bitter line. She looked as if she wanted to hurl her handbag at the ground.

Outside his uncle chopped wood. Timber seasoned for six months.

The axe split the wood in two, then into quarters. He found the checks and cracks easily. Thunk. Thunk. Crisp white sounds.

He stooped and collected the quarters. Then he tossed them and some kindling into the wheelbarrow. He picked up the axe again.

His boots crunched through the dirt. As he moved around the woodblock, his steps were shuffling and deliberate. Like a bridegroom practicing his wedding steps.

Step forward. Step back. Adjust your stance. Swing.

Corridini forgot the sounds were there. When they stopped, he didn't notice. Then the light in the shed changed and he felt cold in his bones again.

His uncle filled the shed door.

'There isn't any future in the past,' he said.

Corridini's ears burned. He closed the newspaper and placed it back on the pile.

After the funeral, Corridini sat in his aunt's kitchen. He wore a little black suit donated by the Salvation Army.

Outside the day grew overcast. A watery sunlight leaked into the room. The colour leached from the linoleum, the teapot, the curtains. Objects became indistinct, their edges dampened and grey.

Wilted on the tabletop before him, looking like a black cortège, lay the clip-on bow tie that he had been made to wear. The air in the kitchen was hot and close, filled with the terrible, suffocating odours of a stranger's cooking.

His aunt stood with her back to him, clattering cups from a cupboard shelf onto the bench. As she moved, she talked. A hard, dry voice, like the bones of a sparrow being crushed. Her eyes assessed him, fierce as crows' beaks.

His battered suitcase stood where his uncle had left it — in a corner by the doorway, held together by two lengths of rope.

Corridini had a memory of it sitting on top of his parents' cupboard. When it was brought down and opened, he was surprised to see how deep and empty it was. His father had carried the suitcase on a boat from Italy, escaping fascists.

Above the suitcase, heavy as a cloud, loomed his uncle. His big arms were folded across his chest like blocks of firewood, and his coal black eyes flared beneath rampant eyebrows, arching at the ceiling as if death itself lurked there.

His aunt's hands were crippled with rheumatism. Her lips became rigid when she lifted the kettle off the stove. After pouring the water, she covered the teapot with a brown cosy. Then she stood at the bench, her eyes closed like she was praying, while the colour slowly returned to her face.

Her avian nostrils twitched. She looked at Corridini with hatred in her eyes.

'How your mother lived was deeply shameful to me,' she said.

'If she was a bint from the gutter, I might've forgiven her. But she was raised as I was, for to love and fear the Lord.'

Corridini's aunt set the table. She wiped her hands roughly on the front of her skirt, then shuffled back across the linoleum.

'People live their whole lives in darkness. Your mother, though, she was raised beneath the same roof as me. She knew the Lord and turned her back on Him.'

Corridini watched her solemnly. She took a jug of milk from the fridge and banged the door closed with her elbow.

'You reap what you sow. Galatians 6. The Lord does not like to be mocked. Your mother could've recited that scripture from the time she was ten. Well, she sowed and she reaped and look what it got her.'

Corridini toted the last of the bags from the toilet block. His shoulders ached and a feeling ran in his veins like sand in a petrol tank. He lumped the bags together on the canvas and used his foot to stop one from tumbling onto the floor. The inside of his head felt as if someone had worked the ridges of his skull with a metal rasp. He pinched his fingers to the bridge of his nose, then turned and trudged to the table.

The naked bulb hanging over the table threw his shadow into disarray. He stood for a moment beneath its glow, his sense of self distorted, confused by the divergence of his shape upon the floor. Moving around the table, he dragged back a seat and sat down. From here he could watch the child as she slept. He lent his elbows on the tabletop and massaged the flesh across his forehead. The child's face was pale as the moon's reflection on a pool of water. He stared at the child darkly.

4
— • —

CHAPTER FOUR

C *orridini's aunt and uncle lived in a ramshackle white house on the southern side of Pine Mountain. Lying at the end of a winding and precipitous gravel road, the front verandah of the house had collapsed years before, and the windows in two of its north-facing rooms were boarded up with buckled sheets of plywood.*

At the back of the house, the land spilled steeply into a gully. There, pondweed clotted the stagnant dam water, and a row of rotted fenceposts followed a disused track halfway up the opposite slope. Fallen bracken and grass tussocks as tall as a man's waist turned what was left of the track into a matter of local myth and conjecture.

Over the years, the gully had been made into a dumping ground. Rifle stocks, car doors and refrigerators had all been tossed or rolled down its slope. In the mornings, a thick mist lay claim to the ground, shrouding the world in a white silence that curled its fingers across the black speargrass and whitened the dark face of the dam, like someone's breath on a broken mirror.

Rising early, Corridini sat on the back verandah, his arms wrapped around his legs, his chin resting on one knee. In the gully the bowed and rusted shape of an ancient tractor blade revealed itself from the mist like a drowned man rising from a lake.

The smell of woodsmoke came from the kitchen. His uncle's boots tramped heavily along the hall. Finally, the screen door opened.

'Your aunt has breakfast ready. You want to get inside before she calls you.'

The screen door clattered shut. Corridini huddled on the step. Small and frightened, he listened as the cracked glass in the windowpanes rattled and his uncle merged into the shadows of the house like a bear into its cave.

After breakfast, Corridini washed the dishes in the sink. Using an upturned crate to stand on, he stored the dried crockery on a shelf in a cupboard over the bench. Then he clambered back down.

His aunt entered the kitchen behind him. She bore in her arms an old leather Bible, its face cracked like the seat of a saddle. She sat at the table.

'Sit,' she said.

Then she dragged the Bible open and began to read.

'The Lord said, 'Shall I hide from Abraham what I am about to do, seeing that Abraham shall become a great and mighty nation, and all the nations of the earth shall be blessed by him? No, for I have chosen him, that he may charge his children and his household after him to keep the way of the Lord by righteousness and justice...'

His aunt paused. The scratched lenses of her spectacles flashed at him.

'Back straight,' she said. 'You've got a spine, use it.'

She returned to the page, found the verse she had marked with her finger, and scoured again the bones of the text like a sear wind.

'Then the Lord rained on Sodom and Gomorrah sulphur and fire from the Lord out of heaven; and he overthrew those cities, and all the Plain, and all the inhabitants of the cities, and what grew on the ground.'

At dinner one night his aunt watched him across the kitchen table. Her eyes were beaded black like a bird's. The skin around her lips turned white.

'What do you say?'

Corridini's face burned. 'Thank you,' he said.

'That's better.'

She kept her eyes on him as he bent over his plate. He picked up his fork and prodded the grey marbled meat with its tines. His aunt put her knife and fork down.

'You don't like roast beef?'

Corridini grew small in his chair. His shoulders hunched, his ears reddened. He mumbled into his chest.

'What's that? You sound like you're subnormal. You're not subnormal, are you?'

The boy shook his head.

'What are you if you're not subnormal?'

Corridini's throat constricted. His heart beat against the bones of his sternum.

'I'm not hungry.'

To this point his uncle had watched silently on. Now, he picked up a dishcloth and carefully wiped one side of his mouth, then the other.

'Your aunt's speaking. Look at her when she speaks to you.'

Corridini dragged his eyes off the plate. The woman peered at him narrowly. Eventually, she sniffed and picked up her knife and fork.

'In this house, you eat what's put in front of you. I can't be at your beck and call whenever...'

Corridini hiccoughed.

His aunt's knife and fork paused, becoming perfectly still.

'Excuse me?' she said.

Corridini hiccoughed again.

He didn't see his uncle's hand move.

A door suddenly slammed shut inside his head. The kitchen went black. Heat radiated outwards from his ear.

In the distance, a muffled thump and clatter. He opened his eyes. The warped linoleum floor stretched before him. His chair lay upended by the meat safe.

Corridini's left ear burned and his eye smarted. He realigned his perspective to the underside of things. To the base of the chair, to the tacks rusted into the chair's upholstery.

His uncle's shoe scraped the linoleum. Without moving his head, Corridini swivelled his eyes. He found himself looking at the scaly skin of his aunt's red knees.

The chair on his left moved. Corridini rolled onto his back. His uncle's dark eyes bore down at him. A vein in the middle of his forehead knotted like a noose.

'You heard what she said to you?'

Corridini nodded.

'Speak when I ask you something.'

'Yes,' said Corridini.

His uncle grunted. He pointed his knife at the boy's chair.

'Pick your chair up and finish your tea. That's the last time we'll be talking about this.'

A month after his parents' death, Corridini rose in the dark just before dawn and dressed by the foot of his bed. He pulled a scratchy woollen jumper over his head and padded down the hall with his shoes tucked under his arm.

At the door to the back verandah, he held his breath. Quietly, he raised the latch and nursed the screen door open. With his heart swollen tight in his chest, he crept into the cold morning air.

Sitting on the back step, he worked his shoes on. When he was done, he remained for a moment with his head tilted to the side. All was quiet behind him. He tugged his jumper sleeves down so they covered his hands like mittens.

Corridini's breath fogged the morning dark. He hugged his arms around himself and made his way towards the dim shape of the gate at the bottom of the yard.

The un-mowed grass brushed his pants legs. At the gate, he released the sleeves of his jumper to fumble the cold chain off its post. Dew seeped through his shoes into his socks.

Visible on the opposite slope was a dark stand of gum trees. In the sky above them, a few scant stars glimmered like rain on a car's windshield. Corridini shifted the gate open and slipped out of the yard.

Crossing the gully, he fell twice near the dam. With mist curling around him, he could barely see more than a few yards ahead. Runic shapes, angular and predatory, lurked in the gloom.

WWII Marston mats. Bicycle rims. A piece of farm machinery, the purpose of which had been lost to time.

In one of his falls, he gouged a divot from his knee. As he struggled out of the gully, the blood stiffened and hardened on his leg. Speargrass grew to his waist, then to his chest. Bugs crawled on his neck. His pants were wet, his shoes caked and weighted with mud.

A half-hour later, he neared the ridge. The sky paled overhead. Here and there pieces of faded colour could be glimpsed through the black leaves where the dawn bled into the sky like a rag wrung into water.

Corridini stopped and sucked air into his lungs. Then he used the snapped end of a dead branch to scrape what was left of the mud off his shoes.

When he reached the top of the ridge, Corridini looked back at the house.

From a distance it seemed small and unremarkable. The windows along the top floor were shuttered and the screen door on the verandah remained as he had left it. A thin ribbon of smoke twisted from the chimney pipe over the kitchen.

Then his breath caught in his throat.

Clearly visible from the back verandah was the path he'd made through the wet grass. It ran from the gate like a chalk mark. At the bottom of the gully, the dark green furrow disappeared into the mist, but he knew with sick certainty it would appear again on the other side.

A jagged green line signposting every step he'd taken since leaving the house.

Corridini started to run. He jogged across the ground with trees rearing either side of him. The land rose and fell beneath his feet like a funhouse floor. He stumbled, regathered himself, went on. The world lurched and careened. Scraps of pinkish sky flitted between the trees like birds. Branches lashed him, snagged his shirt, whipped his legs, caught his arms. One struck him near the nose and lip. Flinging his hands up, he sprawled headlong into the dirt and bramble. Sobbing now, he scrambled upright and blundered on.

He ran a hundred yards then collapsed at the edge of a clearing. Wedging himself against the base of a tree, he rolled into a tight ball and felt the sharp-edged gravel on the ground indent itself into his cheek. When he shifted, bits of gravel rose with him. He brushed them away, leaving blood-dotted gnomic inscriptions imprinted like ragged teeth marks in his flesh.

An ant traversed the terrain of his jumper sleeve, navigating the woollen folds with singleness of purpose. It abandoned his jumper for the back of his hand and tickled across his knuckle and the crook of his resting finger. He sniffled snot into his head. A resigned calm settled over him. His tears dried in two crusted lines on his cheek.

When the ant reached the quick of his fingernail, it paused momentarily, arching its body, quivering. Then it crossed his nailfold and fingertip and disappeared into the litter of dead leaves around him.

Corridini turned onto his back and let his eyes travel the length of the tree trunk. Through the cross-hatched branches overhead, the dawn had been burned from the sky. A piece of bark dangled near his face, turning on the end of a spider's web. It made a strange and mournful carousel.

Without willing it, he closed his eyes and fell asleep.

When his uncle found him, he gripped Corridini by the arm and with no apparent effort lifted him onto his feet like a doll. He brushed the twigs and leaves from the back of the boy's clothes then stood him against a tree. 'Are you thirsty?' he asked.

Corridini didn't reply. Instead, he edged away from his uncle. The old man snagged his jumper. 'Stay put,' he said.

He pushed a water bottle into Corridini's hands. 'Next time, you want to take water with you.'

The boy didn't speak. He grappled with the cap on the bottle.

'You couldn't fight your way out of a paper bag, could you?'

His uncle took the bottle and spun the cap off, then gave the bottle back to the boy. He watched Corridini drink, gulping from the bottle mouth.

Corridini lowered the bottle gasping. His throat and the top of his shirt were wet where the water had spilled. He drank again.

Corridini's uncle scowled. He removed his hat and wiped his brow.

'I don't know where you were headed. In this direction the nearest town is twenty miles. You've managed about a mile, as the crow flies. Still, you live and learn, I guess.'

His uncle restored his hat to his head. As the hat brim settled over his eyes, the black of his pupils went flat and cold.

'Let me tell you something. In America, when Negro slaves ran off, the men that owned them would break their ankles with a block of wood and a hammer. They had a name for it. Hobbling. It was an evil thing to do, but it served a purpose.'

He stood over Corridini for a moment, his jaw working as if he were chewing on something. Finally, he shook his head and turned away. Heading back towards the slope and gully, his step was assured and steadfast. He neither paused nor looked back.

Corridini watched him. Sweat darkened his uncle's shirt in patches. As he moved further away the bushland appeared to swim around him, mottling the faded khaki of his shirt, and merging him into the bush.

A day later Corridini stood in the bottom paddock of a neighbour's farm. Before him creaked the great corpse of a Poll Hereford cow, dangling above its shadow in the dust. The neighbour's name was Claymore. He stood a few paces off and addressed himself to Corridini's uncle.

'Frank's not squeamish, is he?'

'I don't know. Why don't you ask him?'

'Are you squeamish, Frank?'

Corridini didn't answer. He looked at the animal raised by its right hind leg from the bough of a tree. The beast's head was gone. In its place was a red maw like a watermelon halved lengthways. Vertebrae huddled whitely in the meat. Dark blood clotted.

Against the fence a pump shotgun leant. The stock was wired up and there was rust on the barrel. A few feet away lay the cow's head. Its eyes grey filmed, tongue lolling in the dirt. Flies streamed over the nostrils. He stayed by his uncle's side, scratching his arm.

A tractor idled on the verge away from the tree. A raw-boned youth, wearing overalls and a giggle hat, sat in the saddle seat, his leg hitched, watching them. Claymore knelt by an unrolled leather case. He drew a skinning knife with a horn handle from one of the handsewn sheaths and straightened. His knees cracked.

'Hear that?' he said. 'God save you from getting old.'

With the horn-handled knife he cut around the hock just below the chain, then he opened the inside haunches in two long incisions. The flesh parted like a madman's grin. Claymore called the youth from the tractor and made a cut down the cow's middle to its dewlap. Together, they pulled at the hide to create tension, then, with the knife blade flashing, worked their way around the animal until its hide lay in the dirt like a woman's skirt.

Claymore nodded towards the tractor. 'I'll get you to winch her down a notch or two,' he said.

The youth sloped away. Claymore returned to the knives. His knees popped again. He swapped the skinning knife for a shorter blade. As he returned to the upended carcass, he cracked a yellow smile at Corridini.

'Don't worry boy, you get used to this.' Then he signalled to the youth by the tractor. 'Right-o,' he said.

The winch cranked and the chain rattled. The beast jerked nearer the ground. Claymore put a hand on the animal, bracing it like he would a heavy bag in a boxing gym. 'That'll do.'

Around the beast, the smell of blood and the buzzing of flies created a circle of focus. All else was peripheral or void. Using the short-bladed knife, Claymore cut around the anus. He dropped the knife into the dirt and clamped the ring of black muscle between his fingers, then he pulled it out of the carcass and tied it off.

The youth came from the tractor and dropped two galvanised tubs in the dirt near Claymore's feet. Dust puffed off the ground. Claymore hooked one of the tubs with his foot and dragged it under the carcass.

It took him less than five minutes to remove the intestines. He opened the belly up, cut through the fat around the viscera, severed the lot from the back of the cavity and pulled the anus back through the animal's body and out the yawning cut in its belly. Then he lifted the paunch, intestines, and bladder out of the beast and let it slide in a clotted whole into the tub at his feet.

He stepped back and looked at Corridini, then at Corridini's uncle. There was blood down the length of his arms. The hairs on his forearms were slicked and black. He wiped his nose with the back of his wrist, leaving a bloody smear on his cheek.

'I guess he answered my question.'

'You mean if he's squeamish?'

'That's right.'

'Doesn't look like it, does it?'

5

—.—

CHAPTER FIVE

L ate in the morning, Corridini stepped from the garage into the service station's little shop and stopped by the counter. Outside, the bowsers stood squat and sentient in the sunlight. Gilbarco pumps, made by Gilbert and Barker thirty years ago. Covered in dust and fly shit now, they looked like derelicts in front of a soup kitchen.

Sunlight scorched the windowpane. Corridini squinted through it at the road. Peeled lettering and a few old signs fixed to the glass. Golden Fleece. Champion sparkplugs. Corridini's eyes were red rimmed and gritty. Two days' worth of stubble darkened his cheeks.

On the cigarette-burned floor by his bed Corridini kept two books. One was called *The World of M. C. Escher*. The other was a high school primer on art and artists. They were the first books Corridini ever bought that weren't spy novels or westerns. He got both in a second hand shop a month after he stumbled across the Escher print and stuck it on his wall.

In the primer was a painting by Salvador Dali called *The Persistence of Memory*. The first time Corridini saw it, he felt an overwhelming sense of déjà vu. Three clocks melting in a barren landscape. A fob watch crawling with ants. The skin of a sleeping man's face sagging on the ground.

Looking out at the bowsers, Corridini felt like one of those clocks. Time dissolving. Reality bent. All things elementally different to what he'd understood them to be.

His eyes wandered. Out near the roadway, desiccated leaves stirred around the broken mouth of a concrete pipe. The movement heightened his sense of desolation.

A car appeared in the distance, sunlight striking off its windshield. Corridini ducked behind the counter. The car blew by without slowing. He straightened and heard his knees creak in the stillness of the day. The car disappeared around a bend. In its wake it left a ragged trail of dust that drifted across the roadside like rain on a field. Corridini stared through the plate glass window at the sky above the bushland across the road. He opened his mouth and exhaled. Somewhere in the distance he could hear the faint argument of birds spilling through the air like pieces of broken glass.

Three days earlier he'd been sitting at the shop counter when a white Holden Calais pulled into the parking lot. Harrigan was in the front passenger seat. Corridini couldn't see the driver. He put his book down and slipped off his stool. At the door he parted the coloured plastic blinds and waited. Harrigan climbed out of the passenger side of the Calais and crossed the gravel towards him.

'Is that Victor?'

'It is,' said Harrigan. He ducked through the blinds and went along the aisle to the counter. His image showed in the security mirror. All limbs, nothing about him was still. 'Where's Glover?'

Corridini dropped the blinds. 'He's around. Why isn't Victor coming in?'

Harrigan took a packet of Twisties from a shelf, then put them back and chose burger rings instead. 'Too fucking hot. He's Lord Muck in the air-conditioner.'

Corridini came away from the door. 'What's he waiting for?'

Behind the counter, Harrigan sat on the stool beside the register. He tore open the burger ring packet and stuffed a handful of the rings into his mouth. 'He wants you and Lucas to go with him to that Polish cunt's place. The cars are ready to be picked up.'

'Polish cunt?'

'Niculescu. If he's not Polish, he's some sort of wog.'

As they approached the car, Corridini, a few paces behind Glover, saw Victor Keats' hands on the steering wheel. Small red hairs, faintly opalescent skin. A corpse's hands.

Glover got into the front seat. He ran the seat back and fitted his legs into the footwell. Corridini squeezed in behind him. The seats were covered in plastic.

Keats drummed his fingers on the steering wheel. He reached down and started the car. 'Smell that,' he said. 'That's Howe leather. I'll be pissed off if you scuff the seats.'

Corridini arranged himself in the back. The plastic rubbed and stuck to him. He didn't know Howe leather from polyurethane.

They pulled out of the service station and turned right. Keats wore a white cotton shirt and a gold chain. The skin on his face stretched over his facial bones like a surgical glove. Glover peered sceptically at the dashboard. Keats caught the expression on his face.

'Four-speed auto,' he said. 'Power Steering, Cruise Control. You'll freeze your tits off in the air-conditioning.'

Glover wasn't impressed. 'Will it suck my cock?' he asked.

Corridini lent his head against the window. Keats changed gears. Along the edge of the road the loose gravel melted together, forming a red band that snapped tight, then hopped and flickered in the sun. Corridini rested his eyes. The V6 engine hummed in the glass. In his ears. In his teeth.

They entered a stretch of road where the softwood scrub still grew. Vine thicket raced beside the car. Through the latticework of branches the sun shone intermittently. Finally, the scrub fell away, and pastureland opened to their left and right.

They banged across a narrow bridge. Corridini lifted his head. Through his reflection he saw blue sky in the creek water.

Then the pastures and paddocks were gone. Used car lots and furniture warehouses replaced them. Rex's Smash Repairs. Affordable Refrigerators. Billboards and roadside signs jumbled together. Winfield Blue. Tontine Pillows. Jesus Loves You. Corridini watched them flip by. After a while he closed his eyes.

When he opened them again, they were in a tree-lined street.

They passed a progression of mailboxes nodding in the shade. Between the houses, patches of brown river showed briefly. Private boat ramps. A moored yacht. On the far bank, an abandoned wharf.

Keats pulled the car to a stop. 'This is it.'

Corridini pushed the door open. A bolt of slow white lightning travelled up his leg. His foot had gone to sleep. He waited for the sensation to subside, then he climbed from the car and hobbled across the footpath to where Keats and Glover stood by a patinaed metal gate.

Keats removed his sunglasses. He pressed the intercom. 'It's me,' he said.

When the speaker box crackled, somewhere in the static, a baby could be heard crying. Above them a camera whirred and blinked. The gate opened.

They walked along a stone path to the front door. Standing in an open vestibule, Keats ignored the intercom. He rapped his knuckles on the frosted yellow glass pane next to the door. 'Fucking intercoms,' he said.

On the lawn an automatic sprinkler came to life. Water clattered amongst exotic palms. Corridini felt the spray flick across the back of his pants. He stepped into the vestibule behind Glover and studied the rolls of flesh on the back of the bald man's neck.

In the frosted glass, a shadow appeared. It hovered briefly on the other side of the pane, then closed in upon itself and vanished. A lock clicked and the door opened.

Facing them across the threshold was an emaciated man with a braided black beard. He wore a battered motorcycle vest with Nazi symbols stitched into the leather. SS bolts. A Black Sun. The Valknut. The numbers 23-9-20 were tattooed into his forehead. His eyes shone in the folds of his skin like coins in a drawstring bag.

'You got to be quiet,' he said. 'Mihai's got his sister's kid here.'

They followed him along a corridor. 'Those numbers,' Keats asked, 'what's that about?'

The bearded man looked around. 'They're Old Testament.'

'Old Testament what?' said Keats.

'Isaiah. Chapter 9. Verse 20.'

'You got me,' said Keats. 'What does Isaiah say?'

The man stopped in the hall. He said:

'On the right they will devour, but still be hungry. On the left they will eat, but not be satisfied. Each will feed on the flesh of their own offspring.'

Looking beyond the man's shoulder Corridini saw an open door. Inside, a plastic sheet covered an ivory coloured Oushak rug. Clothes pegs held the window curtains closed. In the middle of the room a wooden, straight back chair sat empty. Homemade straps dangled from the chair arms.

Except for a black framed photograph of a plump middle-aged woman, the room was otherwise unadorned. The woman's image hung on the wall facing the empty chair. She sat with her hands patiently folded like a spinster aunt in a doctor's surgery.

The bearded man pulled the door shut. 'Mihai's old bloke uses the room when he visits.'

'I take it he's not visiting now,' said Keats.

'No,' said the bearded man. 'That's why it's empty.'

They turned from the corridor into a large living room. At one end was a modern kitchen and beside the kitchen a wrought-iron staircase. Floor to ceiling glass doors faced a wide verandah.

Hanging on the walls were paintings of rainforest birds and voluptuous flowers. As Corridini passed them he studied the paintings. The birds were primal and vicious looking. The flowers, with their fleshy stamens and petals, were pornographic and unsettling.

Before one of the paintings, a blonde woman wearing a leotard and legwarmers worked out on an exercise bike. Her face was hot with exertion. She had a Sony Walkman clamped to her ears emitting a persistent and tinny buzz. As the men went by behind her, she didn't look around. Something in the way she held her shoulders told Corridini she was sick with fear.

They slid open a glass door.

On the verandah, gazing out at the river, a man wearing a pair of shorts reclined on a deck chair. A baby slept on his chest. The man's skin was deeply tanned and covered with tattooed renderings of an apocalyptic world.

When he saw Keats, he put a finger to his lips. 'We got to be quiet,' he said. 'The lungs on him, you got no idea.'

Keats ignored him. 'Jesus, Mihai, you turned the place into a fucking nursery.'

The man's eyes were hidden by a pair of Porsche Carerra sunglasses. He raised his eyebrows, pouting slightly.

'Please, Victor. You wouldn't say this if you knew what a misery it was getting him to sleep.'

Keats glanced at the baby. Lying on Niculescu's tattooed chest, it looked like it was bedded down on a nest of snakes. 'Where'd you steal it from?' he asked.

'He's my sister's kid,' said Niculescu. 'Three weeks old. You should see the balls on him.'

Keats grimaced. 'Listen, Mihai, I brought Lucas and Frank with me. You want the cars ready Monday, we need to keep things moving.'

Niculescu waved his hand. 'Sure, sure,' he said. 'But right now I'm worried about this kid. They say the sun's good for him, but if I leave him like this he'll be roasted like a chicken.'

Keats looked around. He clicked his fingers. 'Put the umbrella up, Frank.'

While Corridini worked the mechanism to open the umbrella, Keats jiggled the Calais' keys in his pocket. 'We need to get this show on the road, Mihai.'

Niculescu moved his deckchair under the umbrella. He signalled to the bearded man. 'Benny, get Mr Keats his bags.'

Corridini stepped to the railing. On the cement and pebbled drive two 1988 Commodores were parked. A carefully tended lawn overlooked the river. Sandstone steps descended to a pontoon jetty. Under a white pagoda next to the steps a man in jeans and a tie-dye shirt smoked a hand rolled cigarette, watching a converted ferry with washing laid across its deck work its way upriver.

The bearded man returned with two bags. He lifted them onto the table and stepped back.

Niculescu showed Keats his smile. 'There you are, then,' he said. 'The keys are in the cars. We'll see you Monday morning.'

Keats remained at the railing. 'Let's look at the bags first,' he said.

'What's there to worry,' Niculescu said. 'You'll see it when you do your magic.'

'I want to see it now,' said Keats. 'With the five of us here.'

Niculescu contemplated the river. As the angle of his head shifted, the reflection in his sunglasses changed. 'Your job is to put it in the cars,' he said. 'How much there is, that's not for you to worry about.'

Keats nodded. 'Until it gets to the other end. Then somebody says it's short, and people come looking for me.'

Niculescu bent down and kissed the black hair on the baby's head. A moment passed, then he sighed. 'Okay, Benny. Open the bags and show them.'

The bearded man limped forward. He opened one bag, then the other.

'Two point three million,' said Niculescu. 'New Zealand 100-dollar bills. James Cook watermark. The Queen's tiara. Show it to the governor of the Reserve, he couldn't tell the difference.'

He took off his sunglasses and looked at Keats. 'You tell me, Victor,' he said. 'Are we good now or not?'

Hunched in a dark corner behind the counter, Corridini snagged a ring of keys off a board with his finger. Raising his head, he peered along the Formica-topped bench. Outside the bowsers watched the road sullenly. A haze of dust obscured the scrub and the road blistered with a slow white heat. He squeezed his eyes shut and shook his head. Nightmare visions flared.

Bodies in the shower stall. Splinters of bone on the tiles. Glover's hulking form in the parking lot. A sickle of light on his scalp.

'That wouldn't be the end of the world, now, would it?'

Corridini flipped the keys around and pared off two of the smaller ones, keeping them separate from the weight of the others on the ring. He straightened and moved around the counter to the far side of the shop.

A row of refrigerated doors lined the wall. Looped chains held them closed. Corridini moved from one door to the next, snapping the locks open, letting the chains slither to the cracked linoleum floor. He returned along the row. When he got to the first door, he tugged it open. Cool air rushed his face.

Soft drink cans and Orchy juice bottles were marshalled along the top three shelves. Fanta, Solo, Kirks Ginger Beer. Corridini ran his fingers over the cans. Finally, he pulled a Sprite from the shelf and pressed it against his cheek. He held it either side of his neck and closed his eyes.

Wire baskets stood at the head of the aisle. Corridini jerked a basket free and carried it along the row of doors. Packets of luncheon meat hung vacuum-sealed from plastic hooks. Holding the door open with his elbow, he slipped a packet loose and tossed it into the basket. The meat sweated in its plastic wrapping, silver-pearled and glistening. He straightened and shuffled on.

When he was done, he had bread and cheese and milk in the basket. A green apple, two bananas, some Freddo Frogs. He looked at the food and felt his stomach shrink. You got to eat something, he thought.

He set his groceries on the cracked linoleum and ran the clicking chains back through the door handles. Leaving the basket on the floor, he went behind the counter and returned the keys to their place in the shadows. As he pulled himself upright, something about the bowsers in front of the shop caught his eye. He unwrapped one of the frogs and bit it in half. With the chocolate sitting on his tongue, he stared at the pump on the left, trying to remember when Harrigan taped the *Out of Order* sign over the pump face plate.

'Wednesday,' he said. 'Fucking Wednesday.'

6

CHAPTER SIX

When they sounded stop work at five o'clock in the slaughterhouse, the noise of the abattoir fell like the shadow of something mythical. Along the iron catwalks came rubber-booted men, cradling hardhats and sheathing knives. They descended the grated steps in ragged single file, flecked and bloodied, their dark heads bowed in a drizzle of stained white paper caps.

Among these figures was eighteen-year-old Corridini. He clambered down the rusted steps and inclined his head like a swimmer climbing from a pool. Digging plugs from his ears, he stretched his jaw and crossed the abattoir in a grey curtain of steam.

A man in rubber boots and blood encrusted khaki trousers aimed a jet of water across his path. Corridini halted and a rainbow shivered briefly in the spray. As the hose moved on, the rainbow hung limply for a moment then swooned across the concrete. Corridini emerged into the waning sunlight like a nineteenth century felon coming from the fog.

In the yard, he peeled a paper hairnet from his head and balled it in his fist. Tossing it into a blackened drum he walked across the ground to a low shed where he cleaned his knives in an outdoor sink. When he was done, he wrapped the knives in an oily cloth and carried them across to *a low wooden bench. He sat in the shaded angle of the shed's roof. After a while, he unbuttoned his shirt and shook it open.*

Later, he took his knives and honed their blades on the surface of a whetstone he carried. Scouring them with a crescent motion, his nostrils pricked at the tincture of the sharpened steel and oil. At intervals he paused in his work. When he was satisfied, he set the knives aside and sat with his arms hooked around his knees, watching the sun fade across the tattered underbelly of the sky.

At length, he rubbed his face and gathered together his knives. Entering the shed, he approached a urinal obscured in shadow. Its metal face was stained a coppery green. He set his hardhat down and placed his knives inside the hat. Then he crossed to the urinal where he opened his fly.

Afterwards, he collected his things and passed the toilet and shower cubicles to the back of the shed. A bay of lockers stood ranked against the wall. Corridini caught an orange plastic chair with the toe of his boot and dragged it across the floor. He rested his knives and hardhat on the chair, then rummaged in his locker for a towel.

As he turned from the locker, the door at the front of the shed burst open. Three men appeared in the dingy light. One, a delivery driver with badly dyed hair, was pinioned between the other two. They were dressed in bloodied overalls. On their backs, the logo of a meatpacking company. A red devil riding a wild bull, the words 'Keats Meats' emblazoned on a pennant streaming from its pitchfork.

'For fucks sake, you're busting my arm,' said the driver.

When they reached the urinal, one of the meatpackers, an outsized man with a carefully shaved head, punched the driver in the ear. He stood back and watched the man fall to his knees. The second meatpacker lent down and spat in his face.

'You're a fucking sheila, Des.'

At that moment, a fourth man entered the shed. He laid his hardhat in the basin of a metal sink and propped his hip against the sink's rim. The late afternoon sun caught his cropped red hair in a fiery glow.

'I'll give you a second to get your shit together,' he said.

The man on the floor gasped for breath. He cradled his left wrist in his right hand. 'Vic. You know I'd never...'

A strand of saliva quivered on the driver's lip. The red-haired man took a folded handkerchief from his trouser pocket. 'You're drooling, Des,' he said.

Dark blood spotted the tiles between the kneeling man's knees. He accepted the proffered handkerchief.

The red-haired man waited for him to wipe his chin. 'I looked in that truck of yours. Cecil's been a carcass short the last three times you drove his route. Tell me, Des, how many sheets are you working off?'

The man on the ground shook his head. 'Just the one, Vic. I swear it.'

The red-haired man arched his colourless eyebrows. 'You've got a head for numbers, then. Here I was thinking you were just some brainless cunt wanting to fuck me over.'

'Jesus, Vic. If there's a problem with the count, it isn't me.'

The red-haired man studied him for a moment. Then he stooped and raised a sports bag from the floor at his feet. He lifted a drill-like instrument from the bag and hefted it in his hand.

'I think I'd like to sort this out while I've still got my own teeth.'

The kneeling man reared off the floor. His feet scrambled on the tiles. From either side, the meatpackers fell on him. They rode him into the concrete and smacked his forehead twice against the grill along the bottom of the urinal. Then they heaved him upright and braced him on the tiles.

Corridini watched from the slanting shadows by the locker bay. The red-haired man stepped away from the sink. Loosened tiles clicked beneath his shoes. He held the device up for the driver to see.

'You've seen what one of these does to the brain stem of a 2-year-old Brangus bull, haven't you.'

The words came flatly, without the suggestion of a question mark. The driver wrenched and twisted in the fading light. One of the meatpackers seized his hair in a clump and forced his head back. Veins popped on his brow, his eyes bulged.

The red-haired man touched two fingers to the centre of his forehead. A benediction and a blessing. Like a priest at the foot of a dungeon gallows.

'It'll be interesting to see what happens when I tap you with it here.'

Corridini shifted and his foot scraped the tiled floor. The sound ran through the echoing space like a cough. Slowly, the red-haired man turned his head towards the noise.

'Well, gidday.'

'Gidday,' said Corridini.

'I didn't know we had an audience.'

Corridini picked up his towel. 'I was just about to have a wash.'

The red-haired man dipped his head. Thoughtfully, he reached out and stroked the driver's miserable brow. Then he moved through the angled bars of light to Corridini. The retractable bolt gun dangled at his side.

'We haven't been introduced.'

Corridini looked at the towel in his hands. He began folding it.

'I'll let you get on with your business, Mr Keats.'

'You know who I am.'

'I do. A bloke on the floor pointed you out.'

'Is that right? You wouldn't know his name, would you?'

Corridini held the folded towel before him. When he didn't speak, Keats nodded to himself as if a test had been passed.

'You work the knocking box, don't you? Those are good reflexes you've got.'

'They could be better,' said Corridini. 'I've got bruises in places I didn't know I had.'

Keats waved his hand.

'Even the best get kicked. The trick is to avoid the ones that'll put you down.'

Corridini got the impression he could take this one of two ways. He watched the other man's eyes closely.

Keats lifted the retractable bolt gun.

'You know how this works?'

'I've never used one,' said Corridini.

'That isn't what I asked you.'

'No sir.'

The red-haired man looked down at the crude weapon in his hand. He lifted it again, then he let it fall to his side. Shaking his head, he turned his back on Corridini. Halfway down the row of cubicles he stopped.

'Tell me your name,' he said.

Corridini tucked the towel under his arm. His throat felt thick and dry. 'Frank,' he said. 'Frank Corridini.'

The red-haired man rapped his knuckles against the shed wall. The sound rolled along the corrugated iron like thunder. Over by the urinal, the two meatpackers stepped away from the driver. They left him lying on the tiles without a backward glance. As they passed along the row of sinks, one of the meatpackers picked up the sports bag.

Keats waited for them in the doorway. Noone looked back at Corridini. It was as if they'd forgotten he was there.

The hammer and spilt box of nails were on the table where he left them. Corridini set his food basket down. He moved the hammer and nails to the bench, then looked back at the dangling light bulb.

From the pile of garbage bags in the corner, flies buzzed. The stench was sickening. Next to the tarpaulin were the two paint tins he'd turned into sieves. They were black with flies.

He went to the cot where he found the blanket had fallen off the child. He stooped and picked it up. As he straightened, his eyes fell across the girl's tiny figure and something in her vulnerability terrified him.

He slid his hand beneath her and lifted her, lolling like a doll, partway off the cot. Running his free hand over the canvas, he touched the damp surface where she'd lain.

'Oh, fuck.'

He lay the girl crossways on the cot and retreated to the sink. His sense of disquiet grew. He closed his eyes and shook his head. Turning on the taps, he crouched and rummaged a bucket from under the sink. Then he tipped the bucket at an angle under the spouts and watched it slowly fill.

As the water beat into the bottom of the bucket an image of his aunt came to him. He saw her in the predawn darkness at Pine Mountain. The last morning that he spent there.

She entered his room without him noticing.

A floorboard creaked. Shadows shifted. Her shapeless dress appeared next to him.

'Yes?' he said.

'You're leaving,' she said.

He watched the frozen pallor of her face.

'Hmph.'.

She stood mere centimetres away. A palpable presence, felt more than seen. The smell of her clothes. The calm horror of her hands. Her inhalations and exhalations. Her seeping hatred.

'You think you're lucky, don't you?'

He shook his head.

'Well, you are. It was a condition of hers. That we do this, or something like it.'

He kept his mouth shut. Then he closed his eyes and hoped she'd go away. In the blackness, her breathing persisted. The smell of her body, the talcum under her arms. She sniffed the air like an animal.

'You won't forget me,' she said. 'You'll carry what I taught you till you die.'

The words were like a weight on his chest. Each syllable stifled him further. She watched his face on the pillow. When he didn't open his eyes, she lent down and put her face close to his. He thought she was going to kiss him, but then his ear grew warm and she whispered raspingly into it.

'Whoever flees at the sound of the terror,' she said, 'shall fall into the pit; and whoever climbs out of the pit shall be caught in the snare.'

7

_— • —_

CHAPTER SEVEN

*T*welve boys slept along the wall. Above them, four high windows, all jammed rigidly shut, looked down on their bunks. The filthy glass of the windowpanes admitted a murky glow of moonlight.

In the communal bathroom, with its gurgling pipes and broken louvres, a toilet flushed. A moment later one of the cubicle doors opened.

In the eerie moonlight, a fifteen-year-old boy padded across the cold floorboards. He climbed into a bunk at the end of the row and tried to keep his bed springs from creaking.

Two beds away a boy named Ford called out in his sleep. He lay on his side with his facial muscles twitching and Corridini, propped on an elbow, watched him until he went still. At the far end of the dorm, another boy farted.

Corridini stretched on his back. He watched the high rafters of the floor above and listened intently to the shifting sounds of the night. After a while he took a small torch from his bedside table and ducked his head beneath the blankets.

Under his pillow lay the folded pages of a letter. He spread the pages out on the sheet beside him and switched the torchlight on.

The air inside grew close and warm. Corridini read his letter through. When he finished, he switched the torchlight off and threw his *covers back. The winter air touched his face and cooled his skin. He wiped his eyes with the back of his hand.*

'You fucking bastard,' he whispered. 'You old fucking bastard.'

Briefly, a car's headlights lit the windows. Corridini followed the sound of the car into the distance. He imagined the street outside. The dark car passing by the huddled classrooms. The hall where they ate their meals. The Major's quarters with its crumbling redbrick facade. The old paddock with its broken fences and slumbering cows.

After the car's engine had faded from earshot, he turned onto his side and watched the pale glow of moonlight on the wall.

Corridini closed his eyes. Sometime later, he slept.

The Major had given him the letter that afternoon. Standing on the steps outside his rooms, he called Corridini's name and waited for the boy to cross the narrow quadrangle with its brown patches of dead and dying grass. When he arrived, the Major had the letter in his hand. He held it up, but didn't give it to him.

'You weren't in prep.'

Corridini climbed partway up the steps.

'I had to get a book.'

'Where is it? Show me.'

Corridini lifted his hand. The Merchant of Venice. *A school-issued paperback. Third hand, dog-eared, unread.*

The Major straightened his back. He assumed a mournful look. 'If you prick us,' he said, 'do we not bleed?'

Shakespeare meant nothing to Corridini. He looked blankly at the man on the steps. 'No, sir,' he said.

The Major studied his face, then blinked several times in sudden fury. He thrust the letter at the boy.

'You're already late,' he said. 'You want to watch yourself. You're playing a dangerous game.'

Corridini squatted in the dirt at the back of the generator shed. He could feel the heat of the generator on his face and arms. It felt good in the growing cold of the July afternoon.

Putting aside The Merchant of Venice, he slipped a hand down the front of his pants and extracted a crumpled packet of Chesterfields. He tapped a cigarette loose and lit it, then he lent into the chain link fence, watching the tobacco smoke curl through the sunlight like a flag.

After a while he took the envelope from his top pocket. He opened it along the flap with his thumbnail then spread the pages of the letter on his knee to read. His aunt's scrawl was unmistakable. Her writing, first in blue ink, then in red, marked the page like the edge of a broken tooth.

There was no salutation. Just his aunt's handwriting crawling like a line of ants across the paper. He flinched as if she was sitting next to him in the dirt.

When he finished, he flicked the butt of his cigarette away and wriggled his back into the fence. He closed his eyes, then opened them again and sat with his arms hugging his knees, staring up at the polished winter sky.

Corridini retrieved the letter from the dirt. He brushed the pages with the back of his hand, then bowed his head over the lines again and read.

'Your Uncle is dead. I found him Monday morning in the gully, drowned. He did not come for breakfast. There was as much mist in the gully as I've ever seen. It's a wonder I found him at all.'

Her blue pen failed. She continued in red ink.

'Dr Callow called the police. They said he tripped on a tyre rim. Adam had his apple, Jericho had Joshua's trumpet. Your Uncle had a tyre rim. Whatever it was, I saw the white of his ankle bone.

'*The burial is next Friday. It's the Methodists in Abbot's Peak. They're the best of a bad lot. At least your Uncle will not be burned. When you come to the farm at the end of the term, you can see him and pay your respects.*'

His aunt did not sign off. Instead, with her red pen failing now, she scratched out a postscript.

'*The morning you came to us, I broke a brown egg into a pan,*' *she wrote.* '*I covered the yolk with a cloth and waited seven minutes. When I took the cloth away the yolk was gone and in its place was a black lizard.*

'*The lizard was dead. It had blood in its eyes and a row of sharp white teeth in its mouth. You need to know this because the Devil is in you.*'

Corridini stood on the railway platform. At his feet lay the suitcase that had accompanied him to the farm seven years earlier. His uncle stood beside him. The old man turned and spat on the ground. Since leaving Pine Mountain neither had spoken a word to the other.

Across the railway tracks a bird rose over the shunting yard. Corridini's dark eyes shifted to track it. A lone dark shape against a sere and merciless sky. Smokestacks, power lines, advertising hoardings. After the farm, the noise of the station made him nervous. He wiped his palms on the seat of his trousers, wishing the train would come.

'*You right?*' *his uncle asked.*

Corridini nodded. Something had lodged in his throat.

'*No use both of us waiting,*' *his uncle said.*

They looked along the tracks at a spot where the white heat of the day quivered.

'*If there's a problem, you call the Claymores. They'll let me know.*'

Corridini nodded. This time he managed to speak. '*I will,*' *he said.*

At length, his uncle turned away. Slowly, he descended the station steps to his battered utility. He rounded the vehicle and stood with his hand on the door. After a moment he opened the door, then, a second later, closed it again. He returned up the steps to stand at the boy's side.

'You'll heed my warnings?' he said. 'There are deviants in those places.'

The boy nodded.

'It's an abomination. Wherever you go, there's sickness and plague.'

Corridini crossed his arms. He scuffed his shoe against the stone platform. 'Yes,' he said.

His uncle looked along the tracks. The band of white heat still trembled on the horizon. From its midst a train appeared. As it grew closer, Corridini's heart swelled, beating against his ribs and sternum, making it difficult to breathe.

His uncle descended the steps again. This time he took the ute's keys from his pocket.

'You'll be home at Easter,' he said.

Corridini took up his suitcase. When he straightened his uncle had climbed behind the wheel of the utility. The vehicle's engine started. His uncle peered through the windshield at him. Standing on the railway platform, Corridini raised his hand, unsure if he should wave or not. The gesture was awkward, like an unfinished sentence.

The utility swung onto the road. Corridini watched it travel up the street. It passed a boarded-up upholsterer's shop, then an allotment empty except for a fire-blackened caravan, and finally a storage yard where birdbaths and imitation Doric columns stood abandoned in the dust and weeds.

At the T-junction, the ute stopped, halting in the middle of the road as if it had stalled there. Corridini watched with his heart in his mouth. At last, when he didn't think he could stand it any longer, the ute turned into the junction and disappeared around the corner.

It was only then that Corridini realised the train had pulled into the station behind him. As he stumbled across the platform to the rear-most carriage, his eyes filled with tears and he began to sob.

Moonlight spilled across the boarders. At the end of the row, Corridini slept. His hand gestured in the darkness like a drunk's.

'Send someone else,' he said.

In his dream a bolt of lightning spread across an empty field. The world stood frozen, like an x-ray, white on black. He felt at the edge of a vast and desolate emptiness.

His hands and feet disappeared. His head turned black. His soul was torn apart by howling winds.

In the morning, Corridini stood a long time in the shower. He lowered his head and closed his eyes and clasped his hands as he'd seen his aunt do. With water streaming over his head, he gave his petition to God.

'See that he suffers,' he prayed. 'Please, God. Send him straight to Hell.'

Someone banged a fist against the wall.

'Come on, Corridini, you wanker. It's fucking cold out here.'

Corridini crossed to the old hall. Once a WWII munitions building, there was little else to recommend it now. Rotted bannisters, a leaking roof. He squatted in the morning sunlight and waited for the breakfast bell to ring. Around him, boys in grey trousers and collared, short-sleeved shirts gathered. They wore jumpers too thin for the cold.

Through the door, long, black tables and uneven benches could be seen. A picture of the Queen at her Coronation hung on the wall. Beside it, covered in fly shit and dust, a picture of Jesus holding a lamb. The sound of clashing metal trays came from the kitchen.

An oversized seventeen-year-old named Klemper, conjunctivitis swelling his right eye like a boil, bumped into him.

'Hey, shit-for-brains,' he said. 'You're blocking the fucking way.'

Falling back, Corridini caught his elbow on the post's edge. He regained his balance as the bell at the end of the veranda clanged. Corridini watched Klemper's massive head bob amongst the boys surging into the hall. He promised himself that one day he'd stick a butcher's knife between Klemper's ribs and twist it.

Inside the hall, a fat, bearded man called Mallory said grace. Afterwards, the fat man sat beside a cherub-faced boy and buttered a piece of toast for him. He cut the toast into quarters and fed it to the boy like he would a trained bird.

Corridini's stomach felt dry and shrivelled. He put aside his own toast and drank a cup of tea. Then he got up and went along the table to where Mallory sat.

'I'm crook,' he said. 'I need to be excused.'

Mallory wiped crumbs from his mouth. 'I'm not stopping you,' he said.

Out in the pale morning sunlight, Corridini followed a concrete pathway to the other side of the school. A creaking wooden church, built in the 1930s, looked over a small playing field. He pushed through the front door into the vestibule.

The structure shifted and groaned as he moved between the pews. In the end he chose a seat towards the front of the church. The pew wobbled as he sat down. He propped his elbows on the backrest and craned his head.

Corridini closed his eyes. The church creaked like old bones. Outside birds chattered. The sound reminded him of knives being sharpened, of edged metal striking stone.

A voice woke him. In the next row, a square-built, muscular man in priest's robes stood watching him. On the inside of his forearm, three crosses were tattooed. He'd come to the school six months ago.

Corridini clambered to his feet. 'I'll go,' he said.

'You don't have to. You can stay until your class.'

Corridini paused. 'No,' he said, 'I fell asleep.'

The priest made a neutral gesture. 'You can sit here anytime you want.'

Corridini went into the aisle. Halfway to the door, the priest stopped him. For the first time, Corridini noticed the man's face. There were scars webbed across his cheek like a broken windshield.

'Father?' Corridini said.

The priest's face was partially obscured in the broken morning shadows. Corridini turned and walked hurriedly out of the church.

In the early afternoon, Corridini again squatted in the dirt behind the generator shed. Eyes half-closed, he smoked a cigarette. Every now and then, he muttered to himself.

Single words. Half phrases. The tail end of things he couldn't keep inside.

A boy named Laurence joined him. He flipped a cigarette into his mouth and struck a match to it. The chain-link fence swayed against Corridini's back as the other boy slumped against it.

Laurence blew smoke into the air.

'Hey, Frank. How are Ms. McLintock's tits?'

Corridini spat on the ground. 'You sit here, you got to be quiet,' he said.

Laurence smirked. He held the tip of his cigarette over an ant crawling on the ground. 'You reckon this is what God does? Sets fire to things when he feels like it.'

Leaning forward, Laurence dropped a gob of spit onto the ant. Corridini flicked his cigarette away.

'Fuck you, Laurence,' he said.

Two boys were sitting outside the dormitory when Corridini came up from the generator shed. He strode past them and entered the building without looking at either one. A moment later they heard him mounting the steps of the old wooden stairwell to the first floor.

'Did you see what he had in his hand?' one boy asked.

His companion rose. Peering through the doorway at the darkened stairwell, he checked to see that Corridini hadn't snuck back down the stairs. 'I'm stuffed if I know what he'd want a rock for,' he said.

The other boy wrinkled his brow. 'I'm stuffed if I know either.'

Klemper's nose spread sideways. His lip tore open; his teeth dislodged. His eyebrow split along the socket. The only sounds in the room were Corridini's controlled breathing and the blows of the rock against Klemper's head and face. After striking Klemper seven times, Corridini climbed off the older boy's chest and dropped the rock onto the floor. He finger-combed his hair, tucked his shirt into his pants, then walked slowly back down the stairs.

Forty minutes later he was sitting on his bed looking out the window at the square of dead grass that the Major called the quadrangle. Around him the contents of his cupboard were strewn. The fat man, Mallory, was packing his bag. Every now and then, he stopped and stared at Corridini with a look of cringing hatred on his face.

'Well, you've done it now,' he said. 'Yessiree. Look at me when I'm talking to you.'

Corridini pulled his eyes away from the window.

'*The police are coming. They'll know what to do with a savage like you.*'

In the hallway, visible beyond Mallory, was a scrap of bandage left by the paramedics. Corridini eyed it blankly. Footsteps came along the hallway. The Major appeared.

'*When you finish, have him put his port in the bag room.*'

'*What about his bed?*' *Mallory asked.*

'*Strip the sheets, fold the blanket, and roll the mattress up.*'

'*We should thrash him,*' *said the fat man.* '*He deserves a thrashing.*'

The Major looked past Mallory at Corridini by the window.

'*You still haven't got anything to say?*'

Corridini looked at him. His eyes burned.

'*The police will be here any minute. You realise you won't be coming back, don't you?*'

Klemper's blood was smeared near where the bandage lay. Corridini remembered the older boy's sluggish descent down the stairs. When he'd reached the bottom, he lent against the newel, then slowly lowered himself onto the floor.

'*I don't know,*' *Corridini said.* '*I don't know why I did it.*'

The Major took a step towards him. His nostrils flared and quivered. With an effort, he regained control of himself.

Mallory stopped packing. He stood with a white shirt of Corridini's in his hand. His eyes bulged.

'*He needs a hiding,*' *he said.* '*That's what he needs.*'

The Major turned away and moved back to the hall.

'*I'll wait out front,*' *he said.* '*They won't be long now.*'

8

CHAPTER EIGHT

Corridini's head jerked off the table. His eyes blinked wildly at the shuttered garage and his elbow knocked a bottle onto its side. Without thinking, he threw his hand out and caught it before it plunged to the floor.

Fragments of a bad dream scurried into the shadows. He clutched the bottle and tried to piece together the residue of his dream. If he could catch the fragments before they slipped away, maybe he could shift the feeling of dread inside him.

What he remembered was the colour orange and a man in his underwear crying in a public toilet. That, and a crumbling stone tower surrounded by wheatfields.

He set his bottle down and held his hand out to the naked light bulb above him. He felt divided into parts. Arms, legs, torso. A creature fashioned out of dried chamois and twisted bits of wire.

His legs shook. His tongue swelled. His teeth ached.

Later, his hands trembling, he dug at his fingernails with the broken end of a match. Dusty parings of blood drifted to the floor. His face tightened as he watched them.

He dropped the match end and shifted in his chair. A rat darted between the shadows. It moved across the sweating concrete like a small mechanical device, squeaking and rusted.

Corridini straightened painfully from the table. He stared at the clock. The roman numerals confused him.

IV. V. VI.

'Five o'clock,' he said.

Somehow the day had crawled by.

At the back of the garage, the door swung open and Corridini stepped into the late afternoon sunlight. In one hand, he carried an old wooden mop. In the other, a metal bucket that banged against the outside of his leg as he walked.

He struck out across the gravel. His mouth tightened into a hard line. A flash of sunlight through the trees along the western border stabbed at his eyes.

Corridini set the mop and bucket down on the tiled floor of the toilet block. He ran cold water into one of the sinks and put his head beneath the tap. A silver curtain of water broke across his forehead.

In an attempt to calm himself, he thought about the Escher print above his bed.

He imagined himself sitting in a stone room. Above him was a window looking out on a rolling field. He saw himself climbing a set of stairs in the same building. In the sky he saw the sun and moon. All that separated his two selves was a maze of empty rooms. Corridini blinked at his image in the mirror.

'If I was a dog, I'd put a gun to my head,' he thought.

Stripping to his underwear, Corridini entered the shower stall. He took with him a wooden brush and a bottle of industrial detergent, and scrubbed at the tiles and drain on his hands and knees. There were flies everywhere. Crawling in his hair, over his mouth, in his ears. If he cleaned for a month, he wouldn't get rid of the smell on the walls.

Moving crab-like across the tiled floor, he spun the shower taps and watched the shifting patterns in the water as he worked. His eyes were febrile and haunted. He wasn't sure how long he could last at this.

When he finished in the stall, he filled his bucket with hot water and worked his way up and down the length of the toilet block, first with the scrubbing brush, then with the mop. It took him an hour and a half, and when he was done, he pulled his trousers on and set his boots on the ground just outside the toilet block door.

Near the sink, he fetched the mop and bucket and brought them both out into the parking lot. He lent the mop against the toilet wall and in the fading polychrome light pulled his boots on. After resting a moment, he picked the bucket up and tipped the dirty water in a murky torrent onto the gravel.

Without looking back he retrieved the mop and returned across the parking lot. The bucket banged loosely at his side.

Half an hour later, Corridini exited the garage again. This time he stumbled beneath the weight of two loaded garbage bags. Behind him, the lighted row of cobwebbed louvres illuminated the gravel in a dirty glow.

Another sickle moon had risen into the sky.

In his hands, the heavy-duty plastic of the garbage bags was slick with gore. Their weight was not insignificant. Halfway to Harrigan's car, he set the bags down and took a moment to catch his breath. His shadow split three ways on the ground before him.

At some point he had stuffed his t-shirt into the pocket of his jeans. Now mosquitos fed on his chest and arms. He slapped two of them, then retrieved his t-shirt from his jeans pocket and pulled it on.

As he worked the shirt over his head, he caught a flash of headlights in amongst the trees at the edge of the service station. Stooping, he picked up the garbage bags, then crouched and hurried towards Harrigan's car.

When he got to the Corolla, he dropped to the ground and scrambled around to the driver's side. His breathing rasped in his ears. He counted six breaths then peered across the Corolla's hood at the road.

The car had already passed. Its high beam lights were finding spectral figures in the scrubland to the east. Corridini watched the car until the curve of the road took it from sight. Then he slid down the side of the Corolla and closed his eyes.

'Where is he?' Keats asked.

'Out back,' said Corridini.

'In the yard?'

'No. The verandah.'

The two men stood on the step. It was early Sunday evening, twelve days before Corridini knocked a hole in Harrigan's skull. The house was Harrigan's rented Queenslander.

'You spoke to him?' Keats asked.

'No,' said Corridini. 'He's shitfaced. We let him sleep till you arrived.'

'Tell me where the girl is.'

'She's in the lounge. Watching TV.'

Parked near the driveway was a yellow cab. In the backseat, craning her head, Harrigan's ex peered out at them. Keats sat down on the top step. He took off his sunglasses and pointed them at the cab.

'Get Raelene and stick her in your car,' he said. 'I'll wait for you here.'

Corridini left the front steps. He went out to the cab and opened the rear door.

'Raelene,' he said.

'Fuck, Frank. Even I didn't know he could be so crazy.'

'Victor will talk to him. You'll be alright.'

'Something's got to be done. I can't live like this.'

'We'll sort it.'

'You don't understand. He grabbed her from the front yard. If I hadn't been there, I might've rung the cops.'

'Not the cops, Rae. You know that.'

Corridini took her arm and guided her from the taxi. Holding her wrist, he turned back into the cab and dropped a fifty dollar note onto the seat.

The driver took the money and folded it into his pocket.

'Right you are, mate,' he said.

Corridini led Raelene to the side of the house. On a tyre-rutted patch of ground beneath a mango tree his panel-beaten Civic was parked. He opened the passenger door and showed her into the car. As he swung the door closed, she put out her hand.

'What about Pete?'

He lifted her hand away from the door.

'Don't worry about Pete. Pete's too fucked up to hurt anyone.'

Back at the house, he climbed the steps to where Keats sat. The fly screen door hung from its hinges like a drunk. They manoeuvred it aside and stepped into the hallway.

To their left lay the day room. A bare foam mattress and some dead potted plants. Ashtrays and beer bottles abounded. On the pillow was a headless black shape crawling with flies. Bloody marks streaked the walls on all sides. Keats wrinkled his nose.

'Raelene's cat,' said Corridini.

At the end of the hall, they found Harrigan's daughter curled on an old brown chenille-covered lounge. Her arms were wrapped around a limp rag doll.

A television set flickered in the corner. No sound. Striations of static. Elvis Presley and some Las Vegas showgirls. A Corvette Stingray and an Elva-Maserati.

Keats switched the television off. The girl shrank into the couch.

'Your mum's here,' Corridini said. 'You want to go home?'

At the sound of his voice, the child cringed. Corridini cast his sense of shame aside.

'She said to get your things. Did you bring anything with you when you came?'

The girl shook her head.

'What about the doll?'

The girl dropped the doll onto the floor.

He straightened and moved away from the couch.

'Well, come on then. Your mum's waiting.'

They went along the hallway. As they passed her father's empty room, the child sought his hand and pressed herself into him. He was acutely conscious of her size, of the smallness of her fingers against his palm.

Outside the day room, Corridini adjusted his position, blocking the girl's view into the room. On the verandah, she released his hand and edged past him to the steps. Corridini pointed to the side of the house.

'Go on,' he said. 'I'll be back.'

He returned along the hallway, past Harrigan's room and the lounge, looking neither left nor right until he came to the kitchen. Then he moved across the linoleum floor to the back verandah.

Harrigan lay on an old car seat. Passed out and snoring prodigiously, he wore a stained pair of Stubbies and nothing else. Beside him was an empty rum bottle and two butcher's knives.

Keats stood by the railing. He had donned his sunglasses again and Harrigan's figure showed in the lenses like a cubist distortion of the human form.

'What a fucking maggot,' Keats said.

Glover moved out of the shadows. A sliver of fading sunlight touched the baldness of his pate. Corridini lit a cigarette and drew on it until the tip glowed red. Keats spread his hands on the railing. The three men looked at each other. Finally, Keats nodded.

At this signal Glover seized Harrigan's shoulders and dug his knee into the smaller man's midriff. In the same instant, Corridini took the cigarette from his mouth and crushed it into the bare flesh of Harrigan's sternum.

'Hello, Pete,' said Keats.

An hour and a half later, in the kitchen of his little flat, Corridini cooked three sausages in a frying pan. As the sausages sizzled in their grease, he boiled a potato then mashed it with butter and milk in a saucepan. Afterwards he scraped a dab of English mustard onto the edge of his plate and carried the sausages into the lounge room.

Surrounded on all sides by the burn marks in his carpet, Corridini poured beer into a glass and ate his meal while rereading one of the books he kept by his bed. The World of M. C. Escher.

When he finished his meal, he pushed his plate aside and flipped back through the book to a paragraph he'd underlined six months earlier.

'... his capacity to balance an admiration for perfect forms and stern structures on the one hand with the idea that everything is but an illusion on the other. Once when I was taking leave of him with a few more prints for collection, he said, 'You are now departing with a package of illusions of an illusion'.'

After reading the passage, Corridini picked up his beer and sat watching the moths batter themselves against the covered light over his small balcony.

He was still watching the moths when Glover's car pulled into the driveway. The headlights played across the window, then fell away. A car door opened and closed. Corridini put down his glass. He went into the kitchen and pushed the screen door open.

'I'll make coffee,' he said.

Glover passed through the kitchen into the lounge. He scowled at the tin of International Roast on the bench.

The lid on the kettle began to rattle. Corridini switched it off and made the coffee. He carried Glover's mug into the lounge.

'You want to know about Pete's missus, don't you?'

Glover took the coffee from him and sipped it.

'You dropped her home,' he said. 'Vic wants to know what you think.'

Corridini took a seat on the lounge. Bits of Naugahyde flaked off onto the carpet. He drank the beer in his glass and refilled it.

'What can I say? He killed her cat by swinging it into a wall.'

Glover sipped his coffee again.

'Does she know Vic had a word with him?'

Corridini nodded.

'What did she say?'

'She wants us to break both his legs and cut off his dick.'

Glover curled his lip. 'A woman scorned.'

Corridini lent back on the couch. He nursed his beer.

'What about you? What do you think?'

Glover was looking at the darkness in the window. He blinked and moved his eyes back to Corridini.

'I think Pete'll eat whatever dog food we give him. He's not stupid. If he doesn't, Vic will put him in a car boot and drop him in a hole.'

'Well,' said Corridini. 'We're right, then.'

Glover grunted. He took what was left of his coffee into the kitchen and tipped it down the sink. Leaving the mug on the bench he took his keys from his pocket and opened the screen door.

The moths danced spasmodically around his head for a moment, then he was gone.

9
— · —

CHAPTER NINE

C orridini climbed into Harrigan's car.

Reaching between his legs, he adjusted the driver's seat. An image of Harrigan's face three days earlier in the concave glass of the shop's security mirror bloomed in his head. As it did, the thought struck him that he had come unshackled from the world. That all his frames of reference were rapidly vanishing.

He peered up through the windshield at the sliver of moon hanging over the trees. A sparse reef of bone-coloured clouds circled the moon. The clouds looked like the shattered remnants of an atoll after a nuclear test.

'Jesus Christ,' said Corridini.

On the wall outside the shop the phone was ringing. Twelve monotonous rings, dragging like time itself. Corridini roused himself and stumbled to his feet. The ringing stopped. A short while later, it started again.

He crossed the cement and picked up the handset. A Hustler centrefold had been thumbtacked to the wall. He fingered one of the thumbtacks.

'I'm standing here with my cock in my hand,' Keats said.

Corridini closed his eyes. 'Hello, Vic.'

'You blokes think I've got nothing better to do than to sit around waiting for the fucking phone to ring.'

Corridini worked at the tack head with his thumbnail. He pressed the soft flesh under his nail into the edge of the tack. The small pain gave him something to focus on.

'I found the money,' he said.

'He speaks,' said Keats. 'Well, that's something. I was beginning to fucking wonder.'

'It's all there. What he took.'

'You counted it?'

'Yes.'

The money had been hidden in the first bowser. Thirty-five thousand in counterfeit New Zealand dollars, stashed behind an Out of Order sign that he, Keats and Glover had walked past every day since the money went missing.

The penny had dropped for Corridini in the shop earlier that morning — as he counted back the days to when he first noticed the sign on the bowser.

Harrigan had put it there while they were collecting the money and cars from the Romanian. He knew then what he was going to do. Probably he'd known it from the second Corridini had crushed the cigarette out on his sternum.

Now the money sat on the table in a duffel bag. Corridini hadn't bothered to count it. After pulling the duffel bag from the loosened panel on the bowser, he'd flipped it open, peered inside, then carried the bag back into the garage and dumped it on the table. There it had sat since.

'Where is it now?' Keats asked.

Corridini didn't blink before answering.

'Glover has it,' he said.

Corridini lent back in the driver's seat.

Adjusting the rear-view mirror, he found Harrigan's daughter in the cloistered dark of the car. He studied the contours of her posture as she slumped unconscious in her booster seat.

Shadows whispered across her. Dark wreaths, evil phantasms, poisonous miasma.

'You're telling me he's not there.'

'No.'

'This is like pulling teeth.'

Corridini increased his pressure on the tack.

'Glover's gone home. We're both rooted.'

'Mate, Lucas doesn't get rooted.'

'What can I say? There were things we didn't expect.'

Silence. Nothing but the contained breathing of the two men on the phone.

Suddenly, the thumbtack sprang from the corkboard. It tinkled across the floor.

'What didn't you expect?' Keats asked.

'What?'

'You said there were things you didn't expect...'

Staring at the thumbtack, Corridini concentrated on the pain in his thumb. The lie came without him having to think about it.

'The money was harder to find than we thought. We had to strip Pete's car to get to it. You know what he was like with a soldering iron.'

Corridini reversed Harrigan's Corolla across the parking lot. He aimed the dented bonnet at the road and shifted the car into gear. Within moments the shuttered service station and the eerie light of the sentinel streetlights were fading into the distance.

Up at Pine Mountain, Corridini crouched in the dank, earth-smelling shadows beneath the house.

Overhead, his aunt went room to room, looking for him. Her voice came muffled through the floorboards.

'Where are you, boy?' she called.

Dust sifted through the interstices. It lay on his eyelashes and the hairs of his arms. She went to the back verandah and called his uncle.

The old man came from the shed. He stood at the back step and slapped the brim of his hat against his leg. Corridini strained to hear their voices.

'That wretched boy,' his aunt said. 'That evil whelp.'

'I'll find him,' the old man said.

Already his uncle was moving along the side of the house. He squatted at the small, latched gate leading beneath the verandah.

'It'll be worse if I have to come in and get you,' he said.

The old man waited. Seconds crawled by. Corridini didn't trust himself to breathe.

Finally, his uncle opened the latch. His face darkened, his neck cords bulged. He crouched. The space under the house narrowed. Soon he was crawling on his hands and knees.

Corridini drew his limbs up. He squeezed his eyes shut and listened to the pounding of his heart in his ears.

The old man came on. His hat dislodged and fell to the side. He heaved himself forward on his elbows. Corridini opened his eyes and watched him. Enraged, ferocious. Grunting and heaving like a wounded animal.

A few feet from Corridini, he lunged.

The boy's head banged against the dirt. Floorboards dragged past overhead. He reached for a stump, but his uncle hauled him away and punched him in the side of the head.

Into the sunlight then. The world veered. Hillside, paddock, sky. All swapped places.

He clung to the back door frame. His uncle clouted him across the skull. A ball of black glass exploded in his head.

Inside the house, the hallway jumped and tilted. His aunt appeared from the kitchen.

'Put him in there,' she said.

His uncle dropped him into a chair at the kitchen table. A moment later, an icepack appeared in front of him. Corridini took it and pressed it to his eye.

When he removed the icepack, his aunt was sitting coldly opposite him. She wet her thumb and forefinger. Slowly, she turned through the pages of the Old Testament.

Her spectacles caught a beam of angled sunlight. Dust glowed like silver larvae on the lenses.

'Leviticus,' she said. Her lips appeared to crack open, and a sour breath passed over the tabletop like a stale wind.

'If your gift for a burnt offering is from the flock,' she read, 'from the sheep or goats, your offering shall be a male without blemish. It shall be slaughtered on the north side of the altar before the Lord, and Aaron's sons the priests shall dash its blood against all sides of the altar...'

Corridini followed a narrow road through rural darkness. On a black hillside, lighted windows watched him.

He scratched his neck and the back of his arm. Ghostly images danced among the trees. Manacled convicts, murdered blacks, hanged men in chains.

Fence rails leapt from the bracken. They raced the Corolla briefly, then fell away like beaten dogs.

Corridini gripped the steering wheel. The windshield rattled. So did the dash. Blackness tilted at him.

The moon appeared, then vanished like a magic trick. A few stars trembled in the east. The road jumped and twisted like a fever dream.

Crossing a narrow bridge, a terrible clattering filled the car. As quickly as it came, the clattering ceased.

The road dipped and turned then flattened. On the left appeared signs of roadwork. A barrier of wooden horses and a grader dozing in the weeds.

Houses appeared. Huddled shrubs and paling fences. Corridini came to a set of traffic lights and stopped.

A town's main street was settling in for the night. Only the pub and a fish and chip shop were open.

In front of the takeaway four teenagers lolled. Their shadows criss-crossed the footpath like distorted figures in a nineteenth century photograph.

Outside the pub, an overweight woman in a house dress remonstrated with a drunk man on the footpath. He wore a pale blue safari suit.

The woman tried to take his hand and lead him to a truck parked at the corner. The man shook her off and sat with great dignity in the gutter.

The opposing light turned orange. Corridini checked his rear-view mirror.

A utility had stopped behind him. In the cabin were two men. The driver wore an Elvis Presley haircut and his eyes were so deeply sunk in their sockets, they may not have been there at all.

Corridini's anxiety bubbled over. It itched through his veins and leached into his sinews. He felt it crawling across his fingertips and dripping from his pores.

Leaning across the passenger seat, he pulled his satchel from the footwell. The 9mm lay where he left it. Nestled with his hacksaw and knives, 'locked and cocked' — how Keats taught him to carry it.

The light changed. He drew the gun out and lay it on his lap. Looking again at the rear-view mirror, he saw the man with the Elvis haircut raise his hand impatiently.

Corridini put the car in gear. He travelled through the intersection. Past the teenagers, past the woman in the housedress, past the drunk in the gutter.

As he drove, he flipped the Browning's manual safety off, then he lay the handgun back on the satchel, and covered it with the satchel's flap.

The ute stayed with him.

On the outskirts of town, he drove by an irrigation pump and a cemetery with lichen-stained angels looking across a dark and silent valley.

The windshield rattled again. He worked the clutch and changed gears. Still, the ute's headlights hugged the road behind him.

Ahead, a sandstone quarry loomed. Chalk-white furrows carved into the night, ridged and gaping beyond a barbed wire fence. Corridini followed the perimeter.

After a kilometre, the quarry fell away. All that remained was the impression of a gouged earth. A terrible emptiness like a cancer eating the bones of the universe.

Stones banged against his undercarriage. The steering wheel jerked. Corridini felt the left rear wheel drift across the shoulder of the road.

He adjusted his speed. A second later, the steering wheel found its grip. Gravel sprayed into the dark and the car retook the bitumen.

When Corridini looked again, the ute had disappeared.

The road turned dusty. A streetlight appeared. Then another.

Corridini climbed the on-ramp to a freeway. The car's tyres fell nearly silent as they breathed across the tarmac like a sigh.

He found the child in the rear-view mirror.

Beneath the streetlights, she was cast in sepia tones. Different ages flitted across her face. She looked five years older. Ten years older. Thirty years older.

Corridini's eyes flicked back to the road. The illusion stunned him. He thought about the Escher book by his bed. Land becomes sea. Birds become fish. Ground becomes sky.

He looked back at the rear-view mirror. The girl was a child again.

Headlights came towards him. White beams in random succession.

Corridini's hands dripped with sweat. He wiped them on his trouser legs and fought the urge to duck his face.

Behind him, a police car appeared.

Corridini moved to the left lane to let it pass. Without altering the angle of his head, he reached across and raised the satchel's flap.

The police car hovered in his side mirror. A Ford XE Falcon. White with Highway Patrol markings. The last of the 5.8-litre V8s.

As he watched, it disappeared into his blind spot. Then it reappeared beside him.

The hairs on Corridini's arms trembled like an insect's antennae. His knuckles whitened. A thousand details sharpened into focus.

Slowly, the police car drew ahead. Corridini held his breath. When the next exit off the freeway came, he guided the car to the left and took it.

Corridini rolled his window down. He breathed in the smell of manure and dark turned earth.

His headlights traced their way across a two-lane bridge. He slowed the car and rested his elbow on the door. Guardrails overlooked a plunging blackness.

At the end of the bridge, a streetlight illuminated broken bitumen. Gravel crunched beneath his tyres. He hugged the guardrail and peered into the blackness beneath him.

At the end of the bridge, he brought the car to a stop. He took his hands off the steering wheel and rested them in his lap. A hundred metres away the road disappeared around a bend.

A nerve ticked in the pouch of flesh near his eye. He turned and looked back at the bridge. Under its lone streetlight, the bridge looked like the set of a 1950s movie.

Corridini draped a cigarette from the corner of his mouth, then snapped a lighter to it. He put the car in reverse. Swivelling in his seat, he threw his arm across the passenger headrest, and with smoke stinging his left eye, guided the Corolla back to the middle of the bridge.

10

— • —

CHAPTER TEN

Stumbling away from the open hatch of Harrigan's car, Corridini moved like a primitive automaton. Dull-eyed, witless; a preternatural light surrounding him.

At the rail, his shadow appeared in the water below. Seized and tugged by the current, it danced in a silent frenzy. His knees turned to rubber. His stomach roiled.

Corridini set his burden down.

His shadow disappeared from the water. Then reappeared. He rested his elbow on the rail and turned his face to the sly moon.

Sweat on his brow, his breathing like a broken vent. In the water his other self clung to a hidden anchor, strung out, flailing. It looked like a dying circus beast.

His shadow withdrew, then showed itself again. This time a garbage bag swung out from the bridge. Gracelessly, it stamped the water once. The river's current seized it, drawing the glistening black plastic into its embrace. A second later the brown water folded over the bag and snatched it away.

Back at the Corolla, Corridini sorted through the garbage bags. Sweat ran into his eyes and his back spasmed. He stepped away from the vehicle and stood like a fighter who'd punched himself out. His arms weighed like lead, his shoulders burned to the biceps.

He spat on the bitumen surface of the bridge and wiped his face with his shirtsleeve.

Along the eastern river bank a breeze siphoned through the scrub. Part of Corridini's disquiet eased. It felt as if a small door had opened. His arms didn't feel as heavy, his mind not so disordered.

He looked beyond the car's open hatch to the end of the bridge. The road remained empty. He hauled another garbage bag from the pile and moved towards the rail with stiff methodical steps.

Three years after his uncle died, Corridini spent the Easter weekend sleeping in a boatshed next to the mangroves at the foot of an old cemetery.

He discovered the boatshed by accident. After getting off a bus at random, he found himself outside the cemetery gates. With no real thought in mind, he wended his way through the century-old graves and saw the boatshed roof through a stand of trees by the river.

He dumped his belongings in a corner of the shed, then covered them with rotted planks and a mouldering life vest. Afterwards, he sat on a stone wall by the mangroves, looking out at the dark shapes moving on the river.

When night fell, he dragged a tarpaulin across his shoulders. The tide was low and the mangroves stank. Somewhere in the dark a fish jumped. He slept in a tracksuit and kept his shoes on.

The clothes he wore, plus three shirts, some underwear, and a pair of trousers, were all he'd brought from the boys' home. One of the brothers had packed them for him just before he left. He remembered standing under a harsh white light as the brother pushed the bag across a wooden counter toward him.

'You can't click it closed,' the brother said.

Corridini put his hand on the bag. 'There was a belt,' he said. 'My father's.'

'Well, I don't see one now.' The brother produced a cardboard box from under the counter. 'You can put your things in here, if you like.'

Corridini ignored the box. He picked the old bag up and tucked it under his arm. 'I'll manage,' he said.

The brother looked doubtful. 'Suit yourself,' he said.

On Good Friday, Corridini made his morning meal out of bread and fruit. He ate his breakfast on the stone wall, still with the tarp around his shoulders. To someone watching from afar, he was a purple shadow set against the river. Shrouded, mystical. Like an acolyte before the dawn.

Later, he pushed away the tarpaulin and sat with his arms rested on his knees. The sun crept through the tree branches and spread its arms across the sky. Corridini turned his face to it.

Across the river a few cars rambled. Spaced at intervals, they looked like rough stitching. He thought about his aunt and uncle. About the school and the boys' home. There were things he couldn't remember. Empty spaces, holes in time.

When the sun had come into the sky, he packed and stowed his things at the back of the boatshed. A narrow road skirted the cemetery's western edge. He followed the bitumen to the top of the hill, then stood for a moment catching his breath. Finally, he put his hands in his pockets and headed in the direction of town.

Outside an old junk shop, he ducked his head to the flame of a match. When he lifted his head, he found his image in the musty silence of the shop's dark window. His face peered back at him from a century's worth of discarded items. Old cameras, iron bedpans, stiffened black gloves.

He finger-combed his hair, then blew smoke into the pane. His reflection disappeared and he stepped back onto the footpath.

Two streets from the river, he came to a small, facebrick Church. On the footpath a liturgical assistant guided parishioners through a gate to the forecourt. They waited on paving stones beneath a towering bougainvillea.

Corridini followed in their wake. He stood beneath the glaucomic outward gaze of a stained-glass window. Around him old and middle-aged men greeted one another gravely. Their women mingled together on the paving stones like drab little birds on a lawn.

Presently, a priest appeared. With his clerical collar cutting into the folds of his neck, he stood at the gate and examined his watch. A birthmark on his forehead looked like a badly broken egg.

A second assistant, carrying a wooden cross, joined the first. At a nod from the priest, the three men in cassocks assembled beneath the cross and formed a little procession into the church. The congregation shuffled behind them.

Corridini watched them go. After a moment he went up the steps and through the dim vestibule into the nave.

He sat in a pew at the back of the Church. A vague and inscrutable presence. For the next half-hour, he mimicked the ritual of standing and kneeling and sitting. Old rites, past iniquities.

A few sheets of mimeographed paper were handed to him. On them were the words of St John's Passion of the Christ. At the front of the church, oddly shaped in their Sunday clothes, three parishioners gathered: two old men and an owlish-looking woman, her hair pinned in a bun like a matador's slain bull.

All three cleared their throats. The men shuffled their feet like primary schoolers. At the lectern, the priest read the Narrator's role. His voice carried a weary, dispirited note.

Putting aside his sheets of paper, Corridini let his eyes wander to the beamed ceiling. The darkening tragedy played itself out amongst the arched and timeless shadows there. Betrayal, envy, cowardice. A cheap asking price for mortal souls.

Then Pilate took the stage. Unctuous, glib, equivocating. His lines were delivered by the woman with the bun in her hair. She wore a Masonite lizard pinned to her bosom like a battle decoration. As Pilate, she jousted with Jesus and the priests as if they were students in an unruly classroom.

'Behold the man,' she said disdainfully.

And the congregation responded with force: 'Crucify him! Crucify him!'

Without thinking, Corridini picked up the pages of the Passion again. His lips moved in silent accompaniment to the words. Eventually he let the pages slip from his fingers. He closed his eyes and bowed his head and shut his mind to it all.

Outside, he accepted the priest's perfunctory handshake, then went down the steps, and out to the footpath. Across the road, a hunched man in an ancient pinstriped suit sat in an empty bus stop. His bearded chin rested on the worn handle of a walking stick. As Corridini walked past, he lifted his chin and waved him closer.

'What did you think?'

'About what?'

'About that.'

Corridini looked at the church. Already the churchgoers were dispersing on the footpath.

'The story's alright,' he said.

'That's what you think? That the story's alright?'

'I don't know. It feels like a stretch to me.'

'What happens next?'

'What do you mean?'

'In the story, the one you think's alright. What happens after they take Him through the streets covered in blood and piss and shit? After they nail Him to a tree and leave Him hanging until his lungs collapse? After they drive a spear into His liver and watch the poor bastard die.'

Here the old man jabbed the ground with the broken rubber ferule of his walking stick. 'After that,' he said, 'what happens next?'

Corridini eyed the old man uncertainly. Then he shrugged.

'They rolled away the rock. Shazam, the tomb was empty.'

The old man creaked to his feet.

'Show some respect. You were just a guest in those people's house.'

Corridini looked at the sun on the bricks behind the bus stop. In the crumbling mortar between the bricks a wasp nest clung to the furrow like some old wartime pillbox.

'Are you a priest?' he asked.

The old man snorted with derision.

'Lord Jesus, no.'

'You're something,' Corridini said.

'Is that a fact?'

'Everybody's something.'

'That's youth talking. Give it time, you'll see.'

Corridini watched the church's cryptlike doors. The old man tucked his walking stick under his arm and dug in his pockets until he found a wadded piece of paper. He took it out and opened it carefully. In doing so, he revealed a black and white photocopy of a sixteenth century painting, done in the fashion of Hieronymus Bosch.

'Look at it,' the old man said.

Corridini took the photocopy. His shadow passed across the page.

An enormous figure squatted obscenely in a fiery wasteland. Holding its mouth open, the figure vomited the souls of men and women between *its legs. Terrified and naked, they were set upon by beast-headed men with pikes and swords.*

Dogs tore at their viscera. Their severed limbs dangled from barren trees.

'It's Hell,' said Corridini.

The old man shook his head. 'Not that. Of course, that. But Him, do you see Him?'

Again, Corridini examined the paper. In the top left quadrant, a great door, like the armoured gate of a fortress, was bursting open. At the door's edges a blaze of brilliant light exploded. In its glow stood a robed figure brandishing a cross like a spear.

'I see it,' said Corridini.

The old man seized the picture. As he folded it into a tight wad again, his eyes flashed angrily.

'They call it the Harrowing. Christ's descent into Hell. It's in Peter and the Book of Acts. The Gospel of Nicodemus. You can read it, but they'll misdirect you. They don't want you thinking about it. It'd be the end of their business if you did.'

'What don't they want me thinking?'

'That He saved them. That He went down there and saved them. Every last bloody one of them. No matter how filled with evil or depraved they were.'

'All of them.'

'That's what I said. Every deadshit, cunting one of them.'

Corridini moved away from the bus stop. His hands had gone numb.

'You're going,' the old man said.

'I've got to,' said Corridini.

'Remember what I told you.'

Corridini didn't say anything.

The old man called out to him. 'Not even Hell lasts forever,' he said.

From the boot of Harrigan's car, Corridini lifted one of the two paint tins he'd fashioned that morning into sieves. The tin's surface was tacky with blood.

As he crossed to the railing, he held the tin in both hands. One hand under the base, the other steadying the rim. A doomed apostate serving the whims of a lunatic master. At the edge of the bridge, he balanced the tin on the rail and rested. The grit in his shoulders subsided. After a moment, he raised the tin.

In a single motion, he launched it over the rail as if it was a shot put. With his arm extended, and his body angled half over the rail, he watched the tin turn gracelessly through the shifting black night until it struck the river with a soundless spray. There it bobbed joylessly for a time. 'Come on, you big bastard,' he whispered. 'Don't do this to me.'

Finally, the river folded over the tin and claimed it from sight.

In a vacant yard across the road from an abandoned glass factory, he found a patch of ground away from the broken bottles and condoms and sat in the warmth of the sunshine. He closed his eyes and listened to the breeze stirring in the dry grass. When a clock across the river tolled, he climbed to his feet and brushed himself off.

His left foot had gone to sleep. He stamped the heel of his shoe, then moved on.

After passing the old railway shunting yards, he turned beneath the arches of a brick overpass. From there he followed the road to the Grey Street Bridge.

Ignoring the river barge and the moored boats in the brown water, he watched instead the concrete walkway under his feet. Breathing easier now, he followed the cracks in the warm cement and let the dry scrape of his shoes lighten his mood.

At the edge of the river, a group of three men were moving through a weed-choked lot. Among them was a shoeless man with a rough bandage on his calf. They came to a temporary-looking building. One of the three produced a flagon of wine. They sat in the dirt beneath a boarded-up window and passed the wine between them.

Lifting the flagon to drink, the shoeless man spied Corridini on the bridge. He studied him over his uptilted bottle, then, seized with a sudden passion, clambered to his feet and gestured in a wild and incoherent way at the dry dock and derelict warehouses across the river.

Corridini considered what prophecy or curse the shoeless man intended. Then he hunched his shoulders and shoved his hands in his pockets and went on his way. Reaching the end of the bridge, he left the footpath and crossed the empty traffic lanes to the opposite side of the road. Someone had broken a beer bottle on the footpath. Corridini savoured the sound of glass crunching beneath his shoes.

In a doorway he spied a bloodied shirt discarded at the base of a metal door like the mummified remains of a dead animal. He crouched beside the shirt and touched the cloth with his fingers. Some of last night's coolness remained in the material but otherwise it felt stiff and dry.

He dropped the shirt and walked on. Rubbing his fingertips together, he wondered at the refuse left in the wake of people's arbitrary misfortunes. The anonymous traces of suffering that layered the places where people frequent.

Ahead the street was empty. Slowly, Corridini started to jog. Again, the grit in his shoulders and arms loosened. Gradually, he broke into a run.

His feet slammed the footpath and the impact exploded through his legs and into his head. His reflection flashed like a demon in the dark-

ened windows of the closed shopfronts as he passed them. Eventually, he
slowed his pace and stopped.

Corridini returned to the Corolla's open hatch. His mind played tricks on him. Shapes appeared in the scrub at the end of the bridge. Spectres, secretive and malign.

In the orb around the lamplight, a moth jerked crazily like a species of angel gone mad.

Bending forward, he found the second tin and straightened with it in his hand. As he headed across the bridge, Harrigan's voice sounded in his head. 'I see you, you wog cunt. You think you're better than us. You're a sheila's filthy rag, an abortion in a bucket.'

At the rail, he flung the tin off the bridge. By the time it struck the water, he had already turned and was headed back to the car.

In the city, that Good Friday, Corridini walked past the fountain in the square with his hands in his pockets. Across the grass and concrete, pigeons formed a grey carpet. When the tower clock struck twelve, the birds took to the air as if a gust of wind had caught them.

Corridini tilted his head back. He turned in a circle, watching the pigeons lift and fall with the sun behind them.

A shaft of white light caught him in the eye. As he blinked, he saw his father's image outlined against the City Hall.

An agony of longing passed through him. He closed his eyes and tried to hold onto the impression. As soon as he made the attempt though, his father's features disappeared, and in their place came a barren emptiness that expanded outwards like the rings of a dead tree.

Corridini dug a cigarette from his shirt pocket. He flipped his Zippo open, made a flame, then held it to the tip of his cigarette. Trailing smoke, he continued across the bitumen to Harrigan's car. He banged the hatch closed and snapped the Zippo shut.

Less than ten minutes had passed since he stopped on the bridge. He rested his weight on the back of the Corolla and let his head fall forward. A bead of sweat dropped onto the paintwork. In the streetlamp's yellow light, shapes curled and uncurled in the droplet like larval ghosts from a parallel world.

A rough sibilance – half shuffle, half scrape – came from the front of the car. Like a broom sweeping a hard dirt floor.

Corridini stepped to his left. What he saw sent a surge of adrenalin through him. The passenger door was open and the booster seat was empty.

'Fuck.'

Scrsk. Scrsk.

Corridini swung the door closed. Loose gravel skidded under his shoes. He moved along the side of the car towards the bonnet.

11

— · —

CHAPTER ELEVEN

*A*s the tolling of the tower clock faded, Corridini felt the world resolve itself around him. *Where to, now?* he wondered.

Nothing came to mind. All he knew was that it wouldn't be back. Not to the boys' home. Not to school. Not to his aunt on Pine Mountain.

It was as if the complex equation of his life had been scrubbed clean. All that remained was an inscrutable expanse of black slate.

Without thinking, he retraced his steps until he came to the doorway with the bloodied shirt. A few paces on and he looked towards the river.

Ten years ago, there were tram lines here. Different billboards, different signs in the windows. Still, he recognised the place.

He closed his eyes and let the sun pour over him. He could almost feel the pedestrians bustling past. Hear the tram bells ringing. Feel his calves itch beneath his long, child's socks.

Beside him stood his mother, her body emanating warmth, vitality. Her presence so powerful, he could feel it with the hairs on his skin. In the nestling coil of his intestines.

She wore a dress patterned with pink and yellow daisies. Its vividness caused an ache in the deepest part of him. He became a child again.

Lifting his foot, he scratched his calf and stumbled against her. Slyly, experimentally. Just enough to contact the bright flowers of her dress. To feel her body under the cloth. Her waist, her hip.

At that moment, the tram appeared. A great, noise-making beast, disgorging sparks and ringing metal. Corridini raised his eyes.

At the rear of the tram, huddled against the window, sat the haunted boy. Behind him, his father. An insinuating, overbearing presence. Shadowy, vicious, malign.

Time lost its balance. The linear progression of events wavered. Moments overlapped, subsumed and replaced one another.

Corridini forgot his mother. Déjà vu overwhelmed him. Was this a premonition, or a memory?

Above him the boy's head turned. Part of his forehead pressed against the windowpane. Boy watched boy. Ghost watched ghost. Their faces merged in the rattling glass.

A car pulled through the traffic lights, its tyres whispering on the gravel. Corridini came from his reverie. He stood with his hands at his sides. When the vehicle turned into a side-street, he went to a bus stop and sat down.

Cigarette butts and scraps of newspaper lay about. He clasped his hands, burning his eyes into the ground. A terrible loneliness went through him.

'All those years ago,' he thought, 'I saw that kid in the exact same spot. Who knows, maybe at the exact same time.'

A quiver went through his body.

'He could've been my brother. More, he could've been my twin. I saw him and knew him. Everything about him. Jesus, I don't want to think what that means.'

Corridini stood beside the car. Ahead, the rail marked the side of the bridge. Beyond it, the water surged and tumbled. Above the riverbank, the scrub and scoured granite of a small hill rose, hunched against the dark like a gargoyle drinking.

His boot heels quickened over the bitumen. A nerve twitched near his eye. His vision fluttered briefly. He touched the Corolla's bonnet and found the engine cooled. The car felt dumb and obstinate beneath his fingertips.

Corridini saw the girl at the same time he saw the gun. The sight confused and disorientated him. An ugly contradiction, impossible to assimilate.

Simultaneously a crack of white light ripped the air and smoke drifted over the railing.

Corridini staggered sideways. The girl squeezed her eyes shut and covered ears. She lay on the ground in a ball.

Something was wrong with Corridini's leg. A hammer had struck him at the top of his thigh. His pants grew clammy and the light around him changed.

The girl took her hands away from her ears. She looked around at the bridge. The white of her eyes rolled like a calf's.

Corridini put his hand out to placate her. 'It's alright,' he said.

His voice floated away.

'The other day, I brought your mother. Now, I'm taking you home.'

The night seemed to list onto its side. His pant leg was soaked. He fumbled at the bonnet, trying to stay upright.

Somehow the car slipped away from him. He slid down the panel until he was sitting on the road. Then he lent against the wheel hub.

His legs were cold and he couldn't feel his feet. He wondered who it was that shot him. He wondered how he had managed to get shot with his own gun.

On his back, now, he looked along the ground at the gun. With great concentration, he inched his hand towards it.

A vast period of time elapsed. Finally, he snagged the trigger guard and dragged the pistol towards him. He thought about closing his eyes but decided against it. Eventually, the pistol was next to him. He lifted it and lay it on his stomach. Strangely he couldn't feel it there.

Despite the cold creeping into his chest, Corridini attempted to sit up. With supreme effort, he managed to lift himself onto his elbow.

Then parts of the bridge dissolved into nothingness. So did a portion of his forearm and hand. When he looked down at himself, he saw he was lying on his back and sections of his body had become indistinguishable from the bridge.

A pool of blackness spread around him. At the end of the bridge the streetlamp threw a dirty yellow light. His abdomen hollowed out, creating a chasm under his ribs.

More of the bridge disappeared. Nothing lay beneath him except struts and beams. His vertebrae recomposed themselves, becoming rubbery, then viscous.

A giant bird swept down from the sky. When he looked, there was nothing there.

The girl sat beside him. She drew her legs up, kept her head down. Corridini moved his tongue around his mouth.

'That was a loud bang, wasn't it?'

He couldn't be sure if any sound came from his lips. Probably not. Still, the words were clear enough in his head.

'When I was young, I sometimes got frightened. I'd close my eyes and tell myself the thing I was frightened of would go away.'

He turned his head to the side.

'It wasn't true.'

Corridini's voice trailed off. He tried to moisten his lips, but his tongue didn't work. He wasn't even sure he still had a tongue.

Everything became leaden. Heavier than it should have been. The stars were gone. So was the moon. All he saw were clouds with a grey light on them. Corridini shifted his head on the bitumen. His face melted into the bridge. He looked across at the girl and all the things he knew about the world fell away.

At first, they went slowly. Then they left in a rush. As if a cloak had been swept back.

Underneath, his skin glowed whitely. Like a chrysalis, luminous, empty. A house abandoned in the twilight, each room stripped of its fittings. Nothing but the pale light of the setting sun on its walls.

Corridini remembered the city that day. His parents, young and alive. Underneath his feet, the footpath trembled. Overhead, the iron arm of a crane arched magnificently across the sky.

Lightly touching his mother's brow was a single curl of hair. Corridini tugged the seam of her dress. She sorted through her handbag, trying to ignore him.

'For God's sake, Frank. I'm busy.'

On the bridge the girl hugged herself. Above, the sickle moon reappeared. Seasons came and went. Clouds grew around the girl's head. She floated in their midst like a boat on a lake.

Footsteps shuffled near him. From the bridge's missing parts an old man appeared. Discoloured whiskers, eyes leaking discharge. His face, vaguely familiar.

'Nothing lasts eternity,' he said. 'Even Hell doesn't last forever.'

The old man's beard muffled his words. He poked the ground with a walking stick.

Corridini smelled pouch tobacco and kidney disease.

'Think of a punishment,' the old man said. 'Make up a number as big as you can. Next to forever, it's nothing. All you can take from eternity is eternity itself.'

Corridini closed his eyes. He opened them again, or imagined he did.

Shadows flowed across the girl. They rippled like tendrils of ink-black kelp around her throat. The old man had disappeared, swallowed by the echo of his own voice.

In the sky above, stars came from nowhere and compressed themselves into a narrow circle. They looked like dew on an old ground monocle lens.

Corridini plunged backwards. The circle of stars scattered. Abruptly his falling ceased, and the heavens confined themselves to a narrow aperture again.

Shadows teemed, swimming across the bridge like a great school of fish. Behind them the banks of the river succumbed to the wild flow and vanished without a trace. Within moments the trees on the scoured hills had followed suit.

Corridini's eyes grew heavy. They sank slowly back in his head like stones in a still pond. The back and sides of his skull dissolved into a warm paste. Only his face remained. A mask hovering over an ageless mystery.

The child was nearly gone now. Almost consumed by the night. Only the light from the small disc of stars glowed on her face.

Corridini floated closer. A nerve on the back of his hand twitched. Otherwise, nothing moved. Silently, the pistol slipped from his fingers. He did not feel it go.

Corridini stepped outside himself. Into a small impregnable place, cold as stone, that he'd known about for a long time. Ever since he first ran away from his uncle. A place where physical pain could not reach him.

Later, in the boys' home, he had doodled its likeness in the margins of his schoolwork. His knuckles showed prominently, scratching and re-scratching the lines. Small stout boxes, unsympathetic, impenetrable.

In all the years he had made them, not once did he recognise the cold sanctuary evoked by the doodles. The iron womb, the empty vault.

'Sofia,' his father said. 'If you hold still, I can have it out in a jiffy'

Corridini sensed the people moving around him. He looked up as a man and woman stepped along the footpath. The woman smiled down at him and a dimple appeared in her cheek. Her face was hauntingly beautiful.

An orange silk scarf was tied loosely to her neck, it floated behind her like the tail of a goldfish swimming in a tank.

The End

ACKNOWLEDGEMENTS

The author acknowledges the support of Queensland Writers Centre in the development of this manuscript, including the guidance of assessor Ben Hobson, proof reading by Charlie Hester, and the assistance of staff and community.

The author also acknowledges the support of his wife, who stood by him regardless.

ABOUT THE AUTHOR

The author lives with his wife and three-legged dog in Queensland, Australia.